THE WITCH AND THE HANGMAN

/ / / /

J.R. RAIN
&
MATTHEW S. COX

THE WITCHES SERIES

Published by
Crop Circle Books
212 Third Crater, Moon

Printed in the United States of America.

ISBN: 9798698780113

Chapter One
It's Routine Until it Isn't

Weird doesn't even begin to describe my life.

I talk to ghosts, can see people hundreds of miles away, recently made a deal to stop an enraged Aztec god from destroying the world (or at least the West Coast of the US), my roommate is a ghost, I can cast spells... and I've started to *like* radio commercials. Seriously, like totally inhuman, right?

This old guy named Pavlov did an experiment where every time he fed his dogs, he rang a bell. Eventually, the dogs would get excited for food at the sound of the bell even if they couldn't smell any food. Think he called it 'operant conditioning.' Radio commercials have a similar effect on me, but not only to make me hungry. They're my opportunity to do everything I can't do while working as an on-air personality—like go to the bathroom, grab a snack, have a sip of coffee, let out a scream of existential anguish, and so on.

I'll admit, finance and stock market stuff goes right over my head. So I'm not really sure what happened at the station, but someone, somewhere worked out a little money magic. K-RAP is no longer a little fish about to be devoured by a shark. The shark is letting us swim alongside it. The giant radio conglomerate *did* absorb us, but they decided for now not to shut us down and reinvent the entire station. Management isn't exactly jumping for joy these days, but at least everyone's stopped keeping their desks half packed up ready to go.

So, yeah. Can't say I listened to radio much before. The few times I tried had been while driving, and invariably, every station happened to be playing commercials whenever I tried to listen. So, I did what most people these days do —got an Mp3 player. Since I'm working in radio now, I understand why they play long blocks of ads... and I don't mean because the station needs income. My show doesn't have music. Those DJs can eat/drink/pee while song sets are playing. Shock jocks, talk shows, and radio psychics like me spend every second of our live shows talking. So, whenever I get a six-to-ten-minute commercial break, I'm usually sprinting for the restroom or trying to inhale my dinner before it gets cold.

Know what else is weird? Me thinking commercials are a good thing shocks me more than making a deal with an ancient god who damn near drowned the entire staff of the radio station on a cruise.

Imagine a toddler in a bathtub with a toy boat. Now put little tiny people on the boat while the toddler slaps at the water. That's about what it felt like for us. It's too terrifying to think of what *almost* happened. We probably came within inches of capsizing and going straight to the ocean floor. No one on board would have survived. Wolfman Stan has developed a permanent phobia of boats, but otherwise, he seems to be doing all right these days.

Speaking of terrifying, I'm fairly certain my former witchy sister Ivy Tanner exceeded the recommended lifetime dose of angry demigod. She said something about her guardian angel—a guy I've nicknamed Gorgeous George—convincing her to use her free time helping people. If you ask me, she had the crap scared out of her and didn't want to say it. So, yeah. Our trifecta has become a bifecta—yes, I know it's not a word.

Now, I'm hoping the metaphysical poop doesn't hit the fan before we find someone to replace her.

I've been working with my friend Samantha Moon in hopes she might be able to reprise her role in the trifecta... but it seems her being an immortal psychic vampire is getting in the way. When we destroyed the old witch hunter and released all the stolen magic back into the world, she got some of her power back... but getting her up to speed is proving difficult. Millicent likened it to trying to add more lemonade to an already-full pitcher.

In other good news, the K-RAP studio is no longer saturated with an overwhelming sense of doom and despair. Turns out, all the haunting type stuff going on around here came from the angry Aztec god, not actual ghosts. See, a former DJ named Stormy brought back this little idol she stole from a sacred site in Mexico. Nothing pisses off ancient gods like stealing from their temples, right? Speaking of Stormy, the station gave me her time slot. Not the grandest reward for saving the world, but hey, it beats night shift. Honestly, I'm just glad we all made it off the ship alive. That's all the reward I need.

Anyway, the universe has two immutable laws. One: mess with ancient gods, you'll regret it. Two: on Wednesday, someone's going to ask if you know what day it is, meaning hump day. And yes, I do throw things at anyone who does the silly camel voice from the Geico commercial. Wait, I forgot a third immutable law of the universe—marketing departments are never going to refuse a cheap gimmick.

'Hump or Dump,' unfortunately, has become one of my most popular segments. Naturally, since it involves the word 'hump,' the marketing weasels want it on Wednesday for all the 'hump day' pun opportunities. What is it? Simple, really... people on the verge of marriage call into my show and ask me to get a psychic read on their prospective spouse. Then, based on what I see and feel, I give a suggestion to either hump (go ahead and marry) or dump.

Legal has a whole bunch of disclaimers they play before the segment and on every commercial break during the segment stating how my show is for entertainment purposes only and K-RAP accepts no liability for any decisions people make as a result of calling in. We had some douche try to sue the station because I warned his girlfriend he was a danger to her, so she called off the wedding. Dude tried to come after us to pay for all the money he lost on reservations, the ring, and so on.

We won, but after the case ended, legal demanded they play the disclaimers on every commercial break, not just at the start. But yeah, the last thing I want to do is ruin people's lives, so I tend to be a little forgiving unless my read on the soon-to-be spouse is *bad*. I've seen all sorts of weird crap. One guy was in a massage parlor when I had his fiancée on the phone—the kind of massage parlor the cops sometimes raid. He didn't get a happy ending. Another time, I saw a woman robbing a jewelry store when her fiancée called me.

Thankfully, most of the time I spy on someone's fiancée, I'd say eighteen times out of twenty, it's fine. Nothing shocking. 'Bad' stuff is usually a feeling the guy or gal the caller wants to marry is going to be lazy, abusive, break up the marriage in less than two years, or the people are just straight up bad for each other. Sometimes, two perfectly normal, great people simply do not mix when combined. They say love is chemistry, and sometimes putting the wrong chemicals together results in a violent reaction.

Aura color helps out a ton there. I can't *always* make out someone's aura when using distance seeing, but most of the time, an aura comes through after a little bit of focus, especially when the person's energy is potent, or bad. Most everyone has an aura whether they like it or not.

Human auras have two parts, what I call the 'outer nimbus' and the 'inner glow.' The inner glow is a two-to-three-inch thick layer of light that clings to people's bodies, entirely surrounding them. Its color gives clues to the true nature of the person. The outer nimbus is—usually—a fairly thin line of color hovering a short distance away from the edge of the inner glow. It's kind of like a little kid drawing a person then outlining them. This line gives clues to a person's immediate thoughts or motivations. Obviously, the nimbus changes color frequently since it represents the 'right now' mindset of a person, while the inner light is more constant.

So, for example, turquoise. If someone's inner glow is turquoise, it means they're depressed. If it's the outer nimbus, it indicates a temporary feeling of guilt. Also, the shape or quality of the outer nimbus can change based on external circumstances. Normally, it's fairly thin and solid, but all sorts of situations can distort it. If the outline is puffed up, cloudlike and hazy, I know I'm looking at someone who's high on a depressant.

As far as the Hump or Dump segment goes,

I'll usually vote dump if I see auras indicating narcissists, psychos, killers, that sort of thing. Some aura colors make for bad combinations. Like if the caller's got a pink inner glow (a nurturer) and their prospective spouse is muddy green (highly selfish) or dark red (dangerous narcissist), it's a total match made in hell. One of them will spend the entire marriage basically either playing parent to the other or being their servant.

Not cool.

Tonight's roster of callers is pleasantly tame. I distant-see each caller while talking to them about the person they are engaged to, then try to home in on the other person, giving them clues like 'does he or she have red hair' or describe something about them so I know I'm reading the right person. I'd be crushed to break up a couple from reading bad vibes off the wrong person. Gotta be careful to sound reasonably generic on the air, like most other 'entertainment' psychics. If I start describing things too exactly to a hundred thousand listeners, I'm sure some weird branch of the government will show up and collect me for study.

I ask a caller named Jennifer if her fiancée Tamir has big puffy hair and a scar on his forehead. He's chilling at home on a PlayStation, no warning signs in either aura, and get the sense the guy is kind with a playful streak, so I declare them a 'hump.'

Curtis, my producer, thinks people in offices around town have betting pools going on regarding 'humps vs dumps.' As in for any given Wednesday show, there will be X amount of humps and Y amount of dumps. There's even a HoD betting pool here at K-RAP, though no one who works directly with me is allowed to participate.

The next call goes great until Julia gives me the full name of the man she's dating—Jerold (with a J) Blake. Now, not only is it a crime against the universe for two people whose names start with the same letter to marry each other (the crime is more severe if they go quirky and give any kids they have all names with the same letter) this guy is rocking a dark red aura with a gold nimbus around it. A narcissist who's presently angry over being criticized. I dig a little deeper psychically, and get the sense he got into an argument with a medical doctor over Facebook about something he Googled and can't handle being told he's wrong. He's so angry, he's considering finding the doctor and punching him.

Yeah. Dump. Big time dump.

A commercial break gives me a chance to run down the hall to the bathroom.

Honestly, the worst part of the job as a radio personality is having to hurry things up in there. My fault for drinking a giant coffee. Curtis has it covered, though. If I'm not in my chair when the commercial slot ends, he can play another one from the mixing booth while he sends the 'goon squad' to hunt me down. Anyway, I make it back to the studio with twelve seconds to spare, then go through three more callers who all get 'hump.'

And then I get one that leaves me in tears.

The last caller to sneak in before the segment ends is an older woman named Miriam, who wants to know if she should marry or dump her boyfriend, Sterling Greene. Both of them are in their seventies, but their age isn't what gets me crying… they both have black auras—which means they're going to die soon. The outer nimbus hasn't turned black yet on either, so they've got anywhere from two weeks to a few months left.

Considering they appear to be living in the same assisted living facility, I'm sure they're well aware of the urgency. I somehow manage to keep myself from blubbing while speaking on air.

"Yes, Miriam. Definitely… don't waste any time."

She chuckles. "Oh, go on, dear. Don't let my

age put ya off. Make it official. Say hump."

Devon, my sound engineer, and Curtis, both die laughing. Fortunately, they're in the mixing booth and the glass is thick enough they can't be heard on the air. Those two think I'm getting misty-eyed over the 'cuteness' of an old couple in love. They have no idea they're both going to die quite soon. The black aura around Sterling offers no clue what sort of man he is, but I do get the sense he loves her.

"Umm, okay. Yes. Definitely hump." Wow, talk about awkward. I feel so wrong saying it to a frail old lady in a hospital bed.

"Thank you, dear. You're sure?"

"Totally." I stifle a sniffle. "In fact, you should marry him tonight."

"Aww, that's sweet of you. Thank you very much, young lady."

"You're welcome." I sit there for three seconds of dead air—a near cardinal sin for radio.

As soon as she hangs up, I hit the button to play the pre-recorded end-of-segment track. Ten seconds to collect myself. I can break down sobbing later. Curtis sends me an instant message asking why I look upset.

One doesn't go on a cruise and get attacked by a giant stone earthquake god without opening their mind somewhat to the paranormal world. Curtis knows I'm the real deal, so I give him the truth.

They're both going to be dead anywhere from two weeks to three months from now, I type in our instant-messaging thing on the computer. *Black auras.*

He grimaces at the screen in the engineering booth.

The end of the Hump or Dump portion of my show brings mc into the second half of my four-hour time slot. When I'm not doing specific gimmicky segments, I end up taking an array of callers who can be anything from 'fortune telling' sessions to relationship counseling to 'should I get a new job' to astrology. Sometimes, people call about strange stuff like aliens or ghosts. A few of my old regulars from the Psychic Hotline try to call me here, but the screeners have started trying to weed them out since those callers don't understand the difference between radio and phone psychics. As in, they expect they can talk to me for an hour.

I won't say the job isn't fun, but sometimes it can turn into a numbing routine, especially when the caller has weak energy or has a relatively boring or outright strange request, like Sadie wanting me to tell her if her kitchen range is really possessed by the spirit of her dead husband.

By the way, it isn't. But it might have an

electrical problem.

A weird feeling hits me out of nowhere at 7:49 p.m., twenty-three seconds away from the end of a commercial break. It's not quite 'ominous doom,' more like the sense of urgency one feels before opening an envelope containing final exam scores or a reply from a college regarding acceptance.

The 'something important is about to happen' feeling gets stronger when I go live again, hanging over me as I read a paragraph of ad copy for Tiki Taco. I'm not even going to get into the bizarre coincidence of a place with such a theme wanting to buy ad time on my show so soon after dealing with an angry Aztec god, but whatever. Gotta pay the bills, right. And hey, they sent the whole station a free lunch a few weeks ago. Their food is pretty good, so I don't feel like a sellout for pushing it. I'm *super* finicky with Mexican/Spanish food.

"… use the promotional code AllieLopez for five dollars off any order over forty bucks. All right. Time for our next caller." Text reading *Vincente Espina, ghost problem* sits at the top of the inbound call queue showing on my third monitor. I poke the button to put him live. No, the computers aren't psychic. We have call screeners. "Hi, Vincente! You're on the air with Allie. How can I help you?"

While waiting for his response, I open myself to his presence for a psychic connection. It sounds weird to think about psychic stuff and modern technology working together, but having an active telephone connection makes it easier to 'find' someone.

"Hi, yes. I don't usually believe in this sort of thing," says Vincente, with no trace of an accent. "But I've experienced some things no one can explain."

A murky, indistinct image of a fortyish man in a blue button-down shirt, jeans, and cowboy boots appears in my mind. He's thick, but not overweight... someone who clearly works a physical job. For no particular reason, it feels wrong to see him not wearing a cowboy hat. Pretty sure he wears one most of the time when not at home.

"What sort of things?" I ask, still focusing on my connection to him. "Are you having a ghost problem?"

Vincente fidgets. More of the scene around him fills in via distant seeing. A kitchen. Lots of medium browns. Steel sink. He's holding a cordless phone but hovering next to the base unit on the wall as if it had a wire tethering it. "Aye. It's not easy for me to say this, but I have no choice. Something is here, and I think it wants to kill me."

Curtis gives me the double thumbs up. Callers like this are great for ratings.

A sense of distress comes over me... suffocating. "You're having trouble breathing?"

"Yes!" Vincente rubs the front of his neck. "It happened about two hours ago, real bad. I saw an ad for your show on a bus, so I figured what the hey, right? The spirit attacked me again just a few minutes ago when I waited on hold."

I swing my distant seeing around to get a look at his face. Square jaw, thin mustache... and a line of red marks across the front of his throat. "Did you feel anything happen, like a tightness around your neck?"

"Exactly. Like something squeezed me so hard I couldn't breathe. Stopped when I went outside." He glances fearfully at his kitchen, the way someone might do if they suspected a home invader stalked them.

The motion of his head gives me a better look at the line of red marks on his throat... and I gasp. Yeah, sure, I may not be any sort of forensics expert, but there's no mistaking the pattern as anything other than a thick rope.

In an instant, I'm certain Vincente suffered a paranormal attack, and the spirit responsible most likely died from a noose... or is a serial killer who strangled their victims. His base aura appears at last—pale blue. He's a peaceful sort of person. Purple-pink in the nimbus around him reveals he's frightened. I get the notion most of his fear comes from the crack in his skepticism. People don't usually take ghosts and such in stride. Heck, I didn't. The first time I saw Millicent, I nearly fainted.

"I think there might be a hostile spirit in your home, Vincente." I zoom out my view to scope the property. "The feeling I'm getting is a male. Lots of anger."

"Maybe he doesn't want me in the house? The choking stopped when I walked outside."

I nod, even though he can't see me. "It's fairly common for physically aggressive spirits to be territorial and defend their homes."

"How can I protect myself?"

"A few things. Give me a moment to have a look around, okay? You know, psychically."

"All right."

Curtis inserts an obligatory 'spooky sound' over the airwaves to fill the momentary silence. Funny, some people actually use my show's 'doing psychic stuff' sound effect as a ringtone. Anyway, a talk show host not talking is usually a big no-no on radio, but the premise of my show is psychic stuff, so they let me get away with not talking continuously, but I can't stay silent for *too* long.

My vision glides past the door to the front yard. It's a one-story ranch house, mostly surrounded by open space except for a cluster of abandoned buildings a couple hundred feet away inside a chain link fence at the base of a hilly ridge. Looks like an old mining operation. He's out there a few miles east of Edwards Air Force Base in the Kramer Hills. Middle of freakin' nowhere. Barring some long-forgotten battle on the land, the most likely source of an angry spirit in the vicinity is the mining operation. If there's a mine tunnel there, good chance the spirit died.

No sooner do I think it, than my head fills with the notion someone killed him for gold. Also, the urgency clinging to me intensifies. Something about this situation *demands* more involvement from me than a simple few minutes of radio airtime. I'm not, however, getting any specific source of anger or connection between the spirit and Vincente.

"The spirit's anger feels undirected. It may be he used to live in the house or on your land. Try gently reminding him he's dead and the two of you can share the house. Also, ask what's making him angry. If you don't have any electronic recorders, suggest he knock or make noise as a 'yes' response."

"Umm. All right. I suppose I can try that."

A soft beep in my ear tells me I'm almost out of time. "I'm so sorry, Vincente. There's more I feel we need to do here, but we're getting close to the end of the show for tonight."

"I understand. Thank you for at least helping me know I'm not crazy." He chuckles.

Seeing his property—and mailbox out front at the end of a long dirt driveway—gives me an address to work with. I also get his phone number from the call queue display.

Yeah... my urge to help him makes sense now. Vincent isn't dealing with an ordinary bad-attitude spirit.

This one's dangerous.

And I really ought to do something about it.

Chapter Two
Out of the Graveyard

One nice thing about working later in the day: no need to set my alarm.

My first time slot at K-RAP sucked in terms of scheduling. I'd been grateful to have a job after Donna fired me from the psychic hotline, but getting home from work *after* the sun came up would have driven me crazy sooner or later.

Anyway, I'm assigned to Stormy's hours now. My new show is Tuesday through Saturday from 4:00 p.m. to 8:00 p.m. Basically, I have the 'evening commute' shift. I show up at the station usually around noon as I've still gotta do the eight-hour day thing. Radio is awesome, but it's not fantasy land. When I'm not on the air, I'm running around performing various other functions, mostly production assistant or sitting in the electronics room learning how to run stuff. Sometimes, I end up staffing a table at promotional events. Figure it's job security. If, for whatever reason, the big bosses fall out of love with my show, I have a chance to keep working at the station as a tech. Or finding another radio gig elsewhere.

But yeah... so happy not to be on graveyard shift anymore. Since changing my work hours, I usually go to sleep around one or two in the morning, because I don't need to wake up early. The other cool thing about my hours is the traffic's all going the *other* direction (away from downtown LA) when I'm heading into work. By the time I leave the studio, traffic's pretty much nil.

Yeah, it's a little nerve wracking to be a woman driving alone at night in LA, but I have multiple advantages most women don't. First, I can toss fireballs. Well, sorta. I mean, there's more to them than simple fire. A brief puff of flames the size of a grapefruit wouldn't really do much damage to anything. My 'fireballs' are lava based—thank you, Gaia—and have some solidity to them. I've never used one on a person before, but I'd like to think a six-pound magma-cored wad of fire moving at the speed of a fastball pitch is going to surprise the heck out of a mugger a whole lot more than pepper spray.

Second, Millicent has my back. I was almost carjacked once due to being stupid and running low on gas. Had to stop to fill up on my way home and some dude pulled a knife on me. Honestly, I can't imagine the kind of tragedy of poor life choices leading up to anyone wanting to carjack an old Honda Accord, but guess what my luck is like, right? So, Millicent appears right in front of us when this guy has a knife on me. Remember the librarian from *Ghostbusters*? Yeah, she did something similar. I think the dude is *still* running.

Anyway, not the most ideal thing to be driving around alone after dark, but I'm not defenseless. Other than worrying where the trifecta is headed—and now an angry spirit who enjoys choking people—life is reasonably calm.

I wake up a little after ten, still thinking about Vincente.

Millicent has become more of a roommate than a haunting. She's worked out the finer details of drawing power from electrical appliances like my television and computer, which enables her to be 'solid' more often than not. She helps out sometimes cleaning, but mostly spends her time meditating, reading, or watching TV. I can't complain, though. She doesn't generate laundry nor consume food. It's great having her around, and she also keeps an eye on the place when I'm away.

Not that it's really necessary. Beverly Hills isn't what one would call a high-crime area.

After a shower and quick breakfast, I try to call Vincente. He answers after six rings, probably assuming I'm a telemarketer. Hey, I might've once worked as an exotic dancer and later did phone psychic work, but I'll never sink to the level of telemarketing. I do have *some* standards.

"Hello?" asks Vincente, his tone hesitant.

"Hi, it's Allison Lopez. From the radio show?"

He mutters, "Someone's trying to trick me," in Spanish.

"No trick," I reply in Spanish as well. "It's really me. I felt something last night when we spoke on the air. Enough to make me want to *really* help you. More than just a few minutes of radio show."

He chuckles, then switches to English. "Do you call everyone back?"

"No. Only when I get a strong feeling about their situation."

I concentrate on our connection, re-establishing it fairly quick. Second time is always faster, plus there's an electromagnetic path to follow via the phone. He's in a bucket on one of those extending arm things, working on the hardware at the top of a telephone pole. Hard to say where he is, but the area's built up like a proper small city, not open scrub desert like around his house. At a guess, he's maybe in Boron or Kramer Junction. I can't tell if he's working on phones or electrical components, but his hard hat has a Southern California Edison logo, so I'll assume he's there for the power lines.

"Wait just a second," says Vincente. "Is this Reya? Marty put you up to this, didn't he?"

"No, I promise you this isn't a prank from your coworkers because they heard you on the radio. Is this a bad time to call, since you're working on a pole right now?"

He pauses. "Not a bad guess."

"You're wearing a green plaid shirt and a hard hat. There's a beat-up green Jeep pickup truck with huge tires rolling by you sporting a big POW-MIA flag."

"Holy shit," he whispers… then starts looking around.

"No one's got a camera on you. Tell ya what. Hold out a random number of fingers on your left hand, but keep it in the bucket so no one on the ground could possibly see it with a camera… three. Two. Now five."

Vincente looks up.

"No drone, either," I say. "I really am psychic, my friend. Did you realize you had red marks on your neck last night?"

His face pales. "Yeah. I did… how did you know? Wait. Don't answer." He chuckles. "You're going to say 'I'm psychic.'"

"Yep." I grin. "So, do you have a few minutes to talk or is this a bad time?"

"I'm just about done here. I can talk. Give me a sec to switch to hands free."

He plugs in earbuds, pockets the phone, and resumes fiddling with one of the components on the pole. "Okay, so what do you need to know?"

"Tell me about the paranormal things going on at your house," I say. "How long have they been happening? Can you think of anything that might've changed to set it off?"

"I've only been in the place for five months. Weird things started happening the first night I slept in the house. Small stuff at first, feeling like someone was in the room with me. Lights turning off or on. Cabinet doors opening. Thought I heard a little kid laughing outside at night."

Uh oh. When most people hear of a child haunting, they go straight to feeling sad. I get scared. Why? Because it's incredibly rare for them to be legitimate children, and I don't mean it in the sense of kids born out of wedlock. Demons *adore* impersonating innocence to trick people and play games. Case in point: the Jaguar god messing with Stormy and Psycho Sally from the radio station by making them think we had a little girl haunting the studio. Okay, so he's not a demon, but same concept, supernatural beings preying on humans' instinctual need to care for our young.

Actual child spirits aren't supposed to linger as ghosts because it's unusual for a child to have 'unfinished business' or the presence of mind to ignore the glowing tunnel. It took a lot of talking for me to convince Peter Laurie to take the step 'into the light' so to speak. Kids don't have the same hesitation. With them, it's more of an 'ooh, shiny!' and they run right to it. Case in point, Peter's daughter wasn't hanging around as a spirit and she died a *bad* death.

Vincente Espina hearing the voice of a child on his property escalates the situation, especially considering the entity is physically attacking him. This could very well be a demon trying to kill him.

"Mmm. Bear with me a sec. Taking notes." I jot down 'lived there five months' 'hears kid ghost' 'strangulation marks, rope' on my notepad. "Okay… do you know anything about the person who owned the house before you?"

"You think it's them?" asks Vincente.

I frown. "What makes you ask that? Did something bad happen there?"

Vincente closes the hatch on the metal box he'd been working in, then lowers the bucket arm, descending gradually toward the truck below. "The previous owner died there. The realtor didn't have much detail. Bank put it up for sale, just wanted to get rid of it, I think. Place was so cheap I bought it without going there in person, decided based on pictures."

"Hmm. Maybe they had difficulty selling it due to the spirit chasing away any potential buyers who went inside." I tap my pen against the pad, thinking. A demon trying to lure people in wouldn't scare someone off, especially before they could buy the place. I write, *possibly territorial.*

"Yeah, could be. The realtor sounded relieved when I passed on the tour, like she didn't really want to go there." Vincente exits the bucket, then climbs down a small ladder on the side of his truck to the street. "Dang. Maybe I should have gone to check it out first."

I keep tapping my pen in thought. "It's a bit early to give up on the house. Do you know anything about the history of the place?"

"Not really. Only that the former owner died in it. Before I called your show, I Googled how to talk to ghosts, and bought a digital recorder. I actually caught one of them talking. Hang on a sec. Let me get it."

I blink. "You have the recorder with you at work?"

"Yeah. In the truck." He walks around to the driver side door. "Brought it in to show the guys. They think I'm playing a prank." Vincente leans into the cab, pulls a small black device out of a cupholder. "Might not hear too well over the phone but…"

Distant seeing, the original Facetime.

He holds the recorder up to his cell phone. A loud 'background noise' hiss starts. Two seconds later, Vincente's voice comes out of the recorder, distorted due to him having the volume all the way up.

"What is your name?" asks Vincente first in English, then again in Spanish.

Three seconds of silence pass before a raspy, "Zay" follows. The 'ghost voice' is toneless like a whisper and spat out fast. Vincente hits a button on the recorder and replays the EVP twice more. It's only six seconds long, so not a big deal. The third time he plays it, I make out a sound in front of 'zay' making me think the spirit is saying his name is Jose.

"Did you hear it?" asks Vincente.

"Jose?"

"Yeah. That's what I think he's saying, too." Vincente stuffs the recorder in his pocket. "Went around the house for a damn hour with the thing. Ghost didn't say anything else."

Tap. Tap. Tap. I stare at the pen. Yeah, I'm not going to get any answers distant seeing the man at his job site. "There's something serious going on at your house, and I'm worried you might get hurt."

"Me, too." He chuckles. "Scary as hell not being able to breathe. Felt like I was in one of those old movies where the spy comes up behind the bad guy with a rope around the neck."

"Would it be okay if I stopped by the place Sunday or Monday?"

"Yeah, sure. Guessing you need to be there after dark, so either's fine with me."

"Sunday then. Sooner the better."

"I really appreciate it. Would you like to have dinner? Just as a thank you for helping, not a date." He chuckles.

"Sure. I'll see you then."

"Do you need my address?"

I read it off to him.

He whistles, impressed. "Allison, you are the real deal."

"So I'm told…"

Wow. I lean back in my chair after hanging up. Something tells me this one's going to be a wild ride.

Chapter Three
Meant to Be

Millicent takes a seat opposite me at the kitchen table.

She's kind of settled on 'dressing up' as a twenty-year-old lately. When I first met her, she had the appearance of an old woman, Peter Laurie's mother. She's been de-aging herself insofar as looks go, ever since. For most of the cruise, she appeared to be somewhere between fourteen and sixteen. It has to be her trying to connect with me on a closer level, since we've been together over multiple lifetimes going back over a thousand years. Maybe even two. Not sure why she went through a teenage phase, but after rubbing elbows with Ivy and her Hollywood people, it seems Millicent's settled in on 'young starlet' age.

For reasons she's never fully elaborated on, she's decided not to jump back into the universe's soul engine after her last death. My best guess regarding why is we got out of sync. One of my past lives must have been killed unexpectedly, and she outlived me by a good margin. Millicent Laurie had been close to eighty when she died, and her son Peter was older than me by at least ten years.

So, yeah. A ghost's appearance is determined only by their perception of themselves. If a spirit doesn't care what they look like, they tend to appear exactly as they did at their moment of death. If they want to change their outward visage, it's possible. Hence why Millicent has been everything from an old woman to a stunning supermodel redhead to a young teenage girl. Now that I think about it, some 'child ghosts' might even be people who regressed after death and can't deal with it. Just because a ghost *looks* like a child doesn't prove they died young. I mean, if Millicent can appear as an old lady one week and a high-school-aged girl the next…

"Seems you have a plan in mind, dear," says Millicent.

Even though she *appears* younger than me, she still talks like she's my mother. Or older sister. It's bizarre to think about, but in past lives, we literally have been each other's moms. Sisters, too. Friends. Cousins… just about every possible relationship two women can be to each other except for lovers—maybe not the weird ones like second cousin twice removed or whatever. But generally, we've been together repeatedly as our souls spun around and around the cosmic machinery.

Hmm. My 'out of sync' idea doesn't hold up. We haven't always been the same age like siblings, though I want to say we were *most* of the time. Her being my daughter or me being her daughter didn't happen as often as us being siblings or best friends. Millicent told me the peak of our power came one time she, Samantha Moon, and I popped out of the same womb at the same time as identical triplet sisters. We'd been somewhere in the Viking lands at the time. Some people mistook us for the Norns, the three fates. But we aren't. Merely witches. *Earth* witches, to be precise. To hear her talk, that incarnation had been our best. No persecution. Everyone respected us. We had power… and protected the world from darkness multiple times.

Witchcraft is kind of like ice cream, comes in multiple flavors and some of them are horrible. Not every witch is a good person. A handful are benevolent like us. A handful are dark. Most end up somewhere in between, generally out for self-interest, but they vary from nature-loving to sinister. I reserve the term 'dark' witch for the ones who actively try to summon demons or invoke the blackest magic and derive glee from hurting people. Selfish witches who use sinister magic to enrich themselves or harm rivals, but don't *delight* in the pain they cause aren't quite as evil—to me —as the demon-raising ones.

"Not really much of a plan," I say. "Got a hunch this man needs our help."

"Yes, a witch's hunch." She reaches out as if to grasp something off the table. A tea cup materializes out of thin air. Purely for show. When she really wants to taste food, she asks me to eat it and enjoys the flavor over our mental connection. "You should listen. By the by, I have the same hunch."

"Hmm. Good to know." I get up to refill my coffee cup. "It's too early for tea, by the way."

"It is never too early for tea." She sips the non-tea. British people everywhere just cringed. Not sure what would offend them more between fake ghost tea or drinking it willy nilly instead of at 'tea time.'

Whatever. It's coffee time for me. I pour the cup, and let out a sigh. "So, what do you think is going on here? Let me guess, the spirit guardian hasn't said a thing?"

Millicent's weak smile confirms my suspicion she didn't receive any concrete info. Yeah, the 'ghostly cheat code' never shares any good information. Sometimes she gets information from the spirit world, but it never seems to be what I need to know in order to make my life easier. Ugh. This whole 'here to learn and grow' thing is a real pain in my backside. Speaking of said backside, maybe I should insure it like J-Lo. Sure, I may not be shaking it anymore to make money, but I'm still sitting on it most of the day at work. Good thing I have a gym membership.

"Figures." Honestly, expecting Millicent to pluck the reasons Vincente's house is haunted out of thin air is foolish on my part. Nothing is ever that easy. I take a swig of coffee, leaning against the counter. I sit enough at the station. "Do you think we're going to need Sam for this one?"

"I'm not sure." Millicent fidgets at the phantom teacup. "It pains me greatly to say this, but it does not seem likely she will be able to rejoin the trifecta. Her immortal nature has permanently affected her relationship with witchcraft. It is like holding a candle to the sun and expecting it to compare."

I sigh. She's not wrong, and that's what annoys me the most. Sam and I have been working a few times a month on her magic, basically doing the Mr. Miyagi/*Karate Kid* thing. Only, her wax is off more than it's on. Whatever soul memories she has of being a witch in hundreds of past lives are either gone or buried under an avalanche of supernatural energy. She *is* learning some things, but as far as her joining the trifecta goes, she's like the one person in every Zoom meeting who's stuck with a bad internet connection, continually dropping off and reconnecting.

"Yeah." I stare into my coffee. "She knows it, too. I'd expected her to be more upset, really."

Millicent offers a sagely nod. "It is difficult to mourn what you don't remember. In this life, the universe had bigger plans for her than witchcraft. Unfortunately, those plans reshaped the link between our souls."

Okay, sad now. Have to sit. I flop in the chair opposite Millicent. "Knowing you're right and liking it aren't the same. I adore Sam, and I'm totally not giving up on helping her work on magic if she wants to pursue it, but… yeah. I don't think it's meant to be for her to rejoin the trifecta."

"Trust the Universe will bring us what we

need." Millicent sips her not-tea again. Is it weird I smell it? "No, dear. It's not strange for you to smell my tea."

"Why do I smell your... umm, unreali-tea?"

She stares at me, rolls her eyes, then sighs. "Because I want you to."

"Right. So, the Universe put us together in the first place, then pulls Sam away from us." I huff a strand of hair off my face, take a huge gulp of coffee, and set my mug down. "Not sure Vincente has time to wait for the machinery of creation to get around to sending us backup."

"Then we will do our best with what we have."

"Lovely..." Looks like I'm going to spend some time in the Spirit Chair looking for signs before work today.

"Don't forget to pick up a scratch-off ticket when you get gas," says Millicent.

Yeah, there's that, too. Millicent convinced me to do something I never saw myself trying: we invoked a spell to attract a little prosperity. Not out of greed, I swear. Renting in Beverly Hills is *not* cheap. If I lived in like Oklahoma or something, what I'm paying in rent would probably cover two mortgages on nice houses.

No luck yet, but we're not trying to become wealthy. Merely get to a point I'm not two bad months away from being kicked out.

Chapter Four
Moment of Calm

Sunday evening, I drive out to Vincente Espina's house.

He lives a few miles south of Kramer Junction. I take Route 295 to a little dirt road going east into the Kramer Hills. A large sign at the intersection (as much as a dirt trail meeting a paved road counts as an intersection) bears a painting of a little wooden building beneath the words 'Loughton Minerals.' Multiple sheets of paper stuck to the sign appear to be warnings of some kind, but I don't bother looking close enough to read what they say.

I've no interest in the mining company.

The artwork and lettering on the sign makes

me think it went up in the 1940s or 1950s. Upon reaching the fork in the dirt trail where it splits between the mining operation on the left and Vincente's house on the right, I get a good view inside the fence. The buildings look so run down it's unlikely any actual mining operations have gone on there in decades. It's a lot newer than I expected, though. Part of me wants to say the place shut down in the Seventies. No particular reason, just a feeling.

I continue driving the hundred yards or so to Vincente's house and park beside a newish white Ford pickup. The instant I cut the engine and get out of my Honda, it feels like someone's watching me. To make things *truly* weird, the mood isn't at all like an angry haunt. A hopeful anticipatory energy is in the air, kinda like how when I'm waiting for a package to arrive from Amazon, I perk up every time a truck drives down my street. At least the house is giving off dread. That's better. Angry spirits willing to strangle people should be radiating fear and ominousness. Not reacting like I'm a mail order victim they're excited has finally arrived. Talk about psychotic.

Vincente is nowhere to be seen, so the sense of being watched isn't coming from him staring out the window. When he invited me for dinner, the vibe coming over my psychic connection to him felt legit. The guy's simply trying to be nice. Some men like living alone and don't feel the need to hit on every woman who talks to them. It's a refreshing change.

The place is exactly as it looked when I remote-viewed it, a brownish-yellow single-story ranch style house. Not terribly big. Looks like it's had some recent work, like a new roof and a central air unit likely installed by the previous owner. Maybe there's a reason why the ghost is so angry. I'd be pretty damn pissed off to spend the money on central air and drop dead before getting much use out of it.

Anyway, there's no fence around the property or a true backyard, really. Hills start a couple hundred feet behind the building, which is otherwise surrounded by flat, open dirt and scattered scrub. The air here smells like dust and Mexican cooking.

I spend a moment looking around, trying to get a 'read' on the land in sight. Sometimes, if the source of a nasty haunt involves human remains, the location of their body calls out to me. Here, I *do* feel something, but it's not a darkness hanging over a particular spot of ground… it's the watched sensation—coming from the direction of the mine.

Okay. Note to self: check out the mine after I'm done here. Something is obviously going on over that way. Makes sense. Mines are super dangerous. I'm assuming, but it's probably a good bet, someone's died there. Don't think there are too many mines where people *haven't* been killed in accidents. Gold mining in this part of the country used to be super deadly and not only from accidents. Miners, their bosses, criminals, drunks, and so on often got into gun-fights. Where mining towns sprang up, gamb-ling, prostitution, and death soon followed.

And sometimes straight-up murder.

Vincente appears at the front door, giving me a quizzical look for standing outside so long. "Miss Lopez?"

"Hi, yeah. Sorry." I walk over to the little three-step concrete porch. "Getting a feel for the energies in the area."

He grins, backs out of the way. "Figured as much. Please, come in."

The house is awash in the fragrance of taco seasoning. AC is on, but not set too high. "Do you know anything about the mine over there?"

Vincente shuts the door behind me once I enter. "Only what the realtor told me. They shut down in 1972. Something about bankruptcy or the owner committing suicide."

I raise both eyebrows.

"Oh, not here. The guy lived in San Fran-cisco. Loughton family used to have Rockefeller type money, but the son or grandson lost it all somehow. The grandson and great grandson struggled. Great grandson's the one who maybe killed himself."

"Ahh." I jab a thumb toward the mine. "I meant more like has there been any accidents in the mine?"

He shrugs, heading for the kitchen. "Not that I know of. Only the previous owner dying in the house. Don't know about the mine."

Another witch hunch tells me Vincente makes tacos almost every day because they're simple and he's good at it. Doesn't want to learn how to cook a variety of things. Bachelor life. Sure enough, he's making a massive batch and has a bunch of empty plastic containers on the counter waiting to be filled for the freezer. I must rate since I'm getting it fresh. Smiling, I pass on his offer of a beer, but accept an iced tea.

"Thanks, but alcohol dulls the psychic senses. Don't mind a beer or two on social visits, but I'm here to help."

Vincente opens a beer, holds it up in toast. "Appreciate it. Feel anything yet?"

"Only a weak presence coming from the direction of the old mining company. Nothing in the house or around it."

"The spirit only starts messing around after

dark. Guess the ghosts have union rules, too." He laughs.

Makes no sense to me why ghosts are more active at night. As far as I've been able to tell, there's no particular reason for it. Nothing about daylight weakens them. Ghosts—as Millicent proves—do not sleep. I've never claimed to be a scientist, but if I had to come up with a logical explanation for why ghosts always seem to be more active at night, I'd say it had something to do with there being less distractions for the living. During the day, people tend to be busy with tasks, surrounded by a loud world of activity. When things slow down at night, it becomes easier to notice unusual happenings.

Over dinner, Vincente and I chat about random things, starting with the phenomenon of ghosts being livelier at night. He points out ghost stories have involved night time for far longer than a loud, modern world has existed. I mention the notion that we, as humans, have an inherent fear of the dark, likely an evolutionary trait because we are—compared to most preda-tory animals—rather helpless at night. Being on edge when we can't see well helps keep us alive as a species. Increased vigilance and fear, a desire to be hyper aware of the world around you can open extrasensory perception, too.

Anyway, Vincente's 'bachelor tacos' are

surprisingly tasty. Better than I expected for a single guy to make. But I suppose when a guy cooks the same thing all the time, it makes sense for him to become good at it. Practice makes perfect, right? Also, it's not exactly difficult to make tacos. We're not talking beef wellington here. And no, I've never had it, but cooking shows tell me it's insanely difficult to make.

I help him clean up once he's got the vast amounts of extra taco meat packed away. He makes a joke that he doesn't *always* have tacos —sometimes he has 'burritos'. Meaning: same filling, bigger shell. No point saying a burrito is no more complex than a giant taco since I know he's making a joke out of it to pick on himself.

"Wondering now if someone died in a mine accident. Maybe got trapped in a cave in and suffocated." I feel good about my idea for less than two seconds. "Nope. Rope marks. Never mind."

Vincente rubs his throat. "The marks went away a lot faster than they should have."

"Yeah, that's common. Paranormal scratches, bruises, red marks… they all tend to fade away pretty fast." I look around at the walls. "Mind if I check out the rest of the house, see if he's hiding somewhere?"

Vincente gestures at the archway connecting

the kitchen to the living room. "Please do."

I wander room-to-room, calling out in English and Spanish for 'Jose' to show himself and talk to me, announcing I'm here to help. The house isn't huge, consisting of a living room, kitchen, one bathroom, two bedrooms, and this little den-slash-whatever room presently holding a small collection of cardboard moving boxes. I don't blame Vincente for not finishing his unpacking. He has to be wondering if he's going to move right back out.

The house is giving off an eerie presence, but it's mild. My read is a ghost has been here often enough to leave a residual energy, but isn't here right this moment. I sigh at the small stack of boxes, mildly annoyed at not finding a ghost before returning to the hallway.

Vincente's waiting for me in the kitchen, opening his second beer of the night. He smiles over his shoulder at me. "Any luck?"

"Not yet. It's obvious a spirit has been here, but he's not in the house at this moment."

"That's good, I suppose." He turns, leaning against the counter. "Kitchen here might be the best place. They told me the former owner was found dead on the floor, strangled."

Hmm. My attention gravitates toward a spot near the back door. I stare at the relatively new linoleum for a few seconds, then get hit with a brief camera-flash vision of a late-sixties, somewhat pudgy, white guy lying face-down. The bag of trash beside his hand tells me he'd been on his way outside with the garbage when he collapsed. My vision of the dead man is there and gone in an instant, like a still image from a camera painted into my mind's eye on a brilliant flash. A faint whiff of kitchen trash flickers across my nostrils. Can't see his throat to see if he's got any marks. From this angle, I could be looking at a victim of a heart attack. It might be a bit much of me to assume, but he doesn't look like a guy who'd be named Jose. More like a Wilfred or Abner.

"Are you all right?" Vincente sets his beer down, hurries over, and puts a hand on my shoulder. "Looked like you're about to pass out."

Admittedly, the vision came on fast and strong, leaving me light-headed. "Yeah. Just got a hard psychic hit. I saw someone dead over by the door. Probably the former owner."

"Think he's upset with me for being here?"

"Well, if someone strangled him, I suppose it's possible he might be lashing out in the same way. Or, he could simply be giving off radiant emotions to make everyone near him feel like they're dying the same way he did. Ghosts do that sometimes, and it can even be an energy imprint on an area. Like if someone is shot in a house, people there sometimes feel a piercing pain where the bullet struck, even if the ghost isn't trying to be malicious. I'm not picking up a real sense of malice in here like I'd expect to find in a place where a ghost is trying to kill people."

"What do we do from here?"

"I'm sorry this situation isn't cooperating." I chuckle. "Still feeling a strong need to be involved to help you. Can't just walk away even though nothing's going on at the moment. I could hang out for a little while in case he shows up. Another option is for you to call me when things start happening again. Yet another option would be for me to sage the house and see if a protection spell might help."

Vincente twitches at the word 'spell.' He's probably a little uncomfortable over the whole 'witchcraft' thing. He's religious but not the 'goes to church' type. However, there's nothing quite like nearly being strangled by a ghost to open one's mind. "What do you think will work out the best? You said the ghost might not be trying to hurt me on purpose? If that's true, I don't want to be cruel to him, but he still damn near killed me."

"Yeah…" I huff air out the side of my mouth, thinking. "What times have you experienced unexplained attacks?"

"Once at like nine, ten. Another woke me up at three in the morning. That one was last week. Basically, the weird stuff can happen any time after dark. If he's done anything during the day, I haven't noticed."

We spend the next hour or so talking about various things the ghost has done in the house. Vincente takes me around, pointing out doors or drawers he's seen moving on their own, spots he's heard footsteps or seen weird clouds of vapor. The more recent attacks where he's become unable to breathe happened in the bedroom, hallway, and kitchen.

I get a few more brief visions of the same guy from the kitchen, one or two showing a fortyish couple screaming in panic, one of a man who looks Mexican—maybe *he's* Jose?—and another white dude so elderly he makes Lo Pan from *Big Trouble in Little China* look like a —Cobra Kai instructor.

The only thing I know for sure is all of them died in this house… but the visions are imprints, not haunts. That said, I can't rule out that a ghost is responsible for all of the killings, either. After all Vicente had straight up been strangled three different times, and the old man I saw still mostly held onto a trash bag. Who continues holding a trash bag when someone's strangling them?

This isn't exactly routine for me, since killer ghosts are a rarity. Last time I dealt with a supernatural entity responsible for killing people over and over again in a house, the victims hadn't haunted the place either, but—and this is a big but (no, not like J Lo)—that had been a demon. It either ate or destroyed the ghosts of the people who died. As far as I know, a ghost doesn't have the power to devour another soul. Sure, it could theoretically kill a living person in the right circumstances. However, the *victim* would normally be haunting the area... not the homicidal ghost. In my experience, the majority of murder victims stick around because they want their killer to be caught. No real point in lingering about if your killer is already dead, which seems to be the case here; after all, cops don't generally arrest spirits.

Fortunately for Vincente, I'm pretty good at keeping my utter cluelessness out of my expression.

"The spirit could be somewhat transient in that he's not bound to this house," I say. "Based on some other visions, I think multiple people have died here, but none have ended up haunting the place."

"Is that normal?"

"Actually, no."

He nods, running his fingers through his hair.

"Unfortunately, there's nothing more I can do now," I say.

"All right. Thanks for trying at least."

"You have my cell number in your phone already." I smile. "Please call me if or when the spirit returns. If I'm on the air, I can still send someone to help. I have friends in, um, weird places." He chuckles at that. "Otherwise, I'll be here as soon as I can."

"Okay. Appreciate it. Any time limit? If it's three in the morning, should I still call?"

I chuckle. "At that hour, I'd prefer you wait... *unless* you think your life is in danger. Let me do a basic protection spell before I go. If it doesn't help, I can come back with a friend and erect a more powerful magical shield against hostile spirits."

"Is this... satanic?"

"No. My magic comes from an earth-based tradition. It's from the Creator, too... just takes an extra step on the way to Earth."

He smiles. "Okay. Go ahead and give it a shot. I'd prefer not to be choked out again."

"I'd profer you don't get attacked again, too." I start for the door. "Be right back. Need to grab my smudging kit from the car."

"Smudging?"

"Sage. Purifying smoke. We sometimes call it 'smudging' the house to do a cleansing."

Vincente gives me a 'be my guest' gesture.

Hoo boy. Hope this works.

But... I doubt it's going to be as simple as this. Nothing ever is. Not when I receive such a strong feeling of *needing* to help.

And when there are killer ghosts involved.

Chapter Five
Local Legend

Cleansing the house goes off without a problem.

Sometimes, doing a protection spell on a haunted property is similar to whacking a hornet's nest, as in all the angry stuff hiding in the walls comes out to object. Since no agitated spirits manifested intent on kicking my butt, I'm pretty sure the house is presently devoid of hauntings. Depending on how powerful the entity is, my spell is either going to make the walls solid to him so he can't go inside… or reduce his ability to hurt the living. By that, I mean, he'd have to use a large portion of his power simply overcoming my spell so he won't have enough 'oomph' left to affect the physical world.

Once done, I head out to my car for the drive home. As soon as I'm outside, the same feeling someone at the mine is watching me comes on, but there's no one in sight. The mood of the 'stare' isn't aggressive, which is also bizarre. Then again, not every ghost is bad. Some simply exist. Maybe there's a dead miner over there checking me out.

I look in the direction of the Loughton Mine for a few minutes, giving the entity a chance to show itself if it wants to. Out of nowhere, a tremendous amount of panic hits me—like I've fallen out of an airplane without a parachute. The absolute fear I'm about to die takes me to my knees, clutching my chest, unable to breathe. My entire body locks up. I can't move. I can't get away from the thing that's going to kill me. Death is inevitable. My head bounces off the door of my car as I collapse to the ground.

Far away in the distance, a child's voice shrieks, "Help! Please! Don't hurt me!"

I'm probably seconds away from a terror-induced heart attack when everything stops. For a moment, I lay there on the ground gasping for breath. My head is spinning, heart racing, thoughts going around in circles.

Next thing I know, I'm on my feet again and Vincente's holding me upright, asking me if I'm okay.

"Physically?" I rasp. "Yeah. Emotionally, not so much. Something horrible happened on this land."

He lets go of my arms, hovering close to catch me in case I start to fall again. "You maybe hit your head when you fell. At least, that's what I think I heard from my kitchen. Are you all right to drive?"

"More a bonk than a hit." I chuckle. "Didn't fall fast enough to do damage. Wow." I rub the side of my head. "Yeah, I'm fine. Just trying to sort out if something dark is attacking me or if the fear that just hit me is latent."

"Latent?" Vincente opens his mouth to keep talking, but twists to look behind him at a faint ripple of gunfire. It's either quite far away or paranormal. "Did you hear that?"

"Yes." Still not getting any sense of a presence around here, so maybe a couple of morons are firing guns into the sky a few miles away. "Latent stuff is like a recording. When emotionally charged things happen, sometimes people can leave a psychic impression on the land, home, or objects nearby. Caught a reading off the land here so powerful it took me off my feet."

"Anything I should worry about?" Seemingly satisfied I'm not about to faceplant the dirt, Vicente stops hovering over me.

"Only if you're psychic." I chuckle.

"Hah. Nope." He smiles.

We chat for a little while, but nothing paranormal occurs. Finally, we shake hands, me promising to return if he calls following any future ghostly activity. I hope in my Honda, give one last look around, then start the drive home. It's frustrating to come all the way out here and essentially accomplish nothing. Worse, my supernatural urge to do something here hasn't gone away or lessened. If anything, it's gotten stronger. Maddening.

When I reach Kramer Junction, I make a snap decision to stop at the city hall. It's not the biggest city hall I've ever seen, but they *do* have a records clerk. A woman in the front room points me down the hall to a plain brown door bearing a gold nameplate reading 'Records – Nick Birch.'

It's already open, so I walk right into a space about the size of a typical grade school classroom. I've never seen so many filing cabinets in one place before. To my right, a hotel-style bell, credit card reader, and several pamphlets sit on a small, wooden counter. A short distance beyond it, a prematurely grey-haired man in his fifties sits behind a steel desk painted 'government green, engrossed in reading something on his computer monitor. A half-height-door at the far end of the counter creates an enclosed area. Since it's obvious non-employees aren't supposed to go any farther into the room, I stand there waiting.

As soon as the man notices me—after I wait like ten seconds—he hops up and hurries over, smiling. "Hello, miss. How can I help you?"

Hmm. I probably should've had an answer for this question ready, right? Honestly, I'm not sure what made me come here. "This is going to sound a little off the wall, but… I'm looking for public records of property ownership." I give him Vincente's address.

"That's not too off the wall." Nick smiles, glances down at the paper he wrote the address on. "Guessing the strange part is *why* you're asking?"

"Yeah. What are your thoughts on ghosts?"

Nick shrugs. "No real opinion either way, but I reckon if you're looking for a haunted house in this area, you've found it."

"Oh?"

"Yes, ma'am." He nods. "This property's seen a whole bunch of bad things. By day, I'm the records clerk. Otherwise, I'm the closest thing the area's got to a local historian, president of the Kramer Historical Society."

"What luck I've run into you then."

He chuckles. "Ain't too impressive. Just me and two ladies from the church."

I rummage my little notepad out of my purse. "Please, tell me everything you know about the place."

"Everything, eh? Well... if I recall, it's recently been sold. The previous owner, Charles Derby, was indeed found dead in the house. Last two owners before him also died there."

While writing the name on my pad, I get another instant flash of the guy lying on the floor next to the trash bag. Okay, he must be Charles. "The other two owners... do you know if they were strangled? Or if marks were found on their necks?"

Nick rubs his short beard in thought. "It's possible. Both cases happened quite some years ago. If memory serves, the police didn't find any indications of foul play like break-ins. Edith and Ralph Larsen owned the house before Charles. Before them, man named Ronald Sanchez. Don't recall anything about strangulation or marks on their necks."

"Okay..."

"No point trying to say one killer's responsible for all of it, miss... if that's what you're implying. The deaths span over a hundred years. The house standing there now isn't the same one Ronald Sanchez owned in the early 1900s. The same killer couldn't still be alive."

I grin. "Exactly. I'm thinking it might be a ghost."

"Say again?"

"The current owner suffered neck injuries that faded away within an hour. Such injuries can be directly caused by spirits."

"Directly?" Nick raises an eyebrow.

"Like scratches or strangling. If a spirit pushed someone down the stairs and they broke their neck, *that* injury wouldn't go away. I'm talking about minor marks on the skin. If my theory is correct, it's possible the red marks disappeared from the victims' necks before anyone found them. The house is kind of... remote."

Nick chuckles. "Yeah, no doubt. Perfect place for someone who doesn't like having neighbors. At least... now. Back when Loughton Mining was in operation, it would've been damn loud. Trucks coming and going all day long."

"I'd imagine so. Do you know why the mine shut down?"

"Sure do. Money James Loughton, the man who owned the mining company, went bankrupt. Place closed down in the early Seventies.

Hadn't been doing too well before him. Been on the ropes since the days of Irwin Loughton."

"Irwin Loughton…" I jot the name down. "And who's he, if you don't mind?"

Nick holds up a 'wait a moment' finger, then retrieves a bottle of spring water from his desk. Oh, this is going to take a while. He swigs a couple gulps, then sets the bottle on the counter. "All right. Let me start at the beginning. Man by the name of Claiborne Loughton struck gold there in 1849. 'Course, by then he'd already become quite wealthy. The gold he found essentially made him the Rockefeller of the era."

"Never heard of him."

"Not everyone with money likes being famous. The smart ones keep it to themselves." Nick takes another sip of water. "He pulled a whole mess of gold out of the ground. Had more money than any man could spend in a hundred lifetimes. As people tend to do, he got old and died, though he lived a damn long time. Depending on which rumor you believe, he made it to anywhere from 101 to 120."

I whistle. "Wow. That's unbelievable…"

"I haven't been able to verify or disprove it. Couldn't find any death certificate for him. Only facts on record relate to his son Wilbur taking over the operation in 1928. Did reasonably well, but soon after Wilbur's son, Irwin, took over, things started to go downhill, and quickly."

"So, Irwin would be Claiborne's grandson."

"Correct." Nick nods. "By the time James Loughton took the reins in 1968, the mining company was a giant black hole in some accountant's ledger. They had a joke going around here back then it would cost the bank more in legal fees to foreclose than they'd be able to sell the land for, so they left them alone for years."

Heh. I chuckle. "Seriously? Or just a joke?"

"Little of both. Nothing's been done with the land the mine's on, other than it being condemned. Bank still owns the property around the mine, but they sold off the residence portion."

"Hmm. Have you ever heard of someone named Jose living there?"

Nick shifts his jaw side to side. "Not exactly. Though, maybe you mean *Hosea*?"

He says it like ho-zay-uh. Weird. Ghost voices on EVPs aren't exactly clear, so it's possible the spirit *did* say Hosea. "Maybe I misheard. Could be Hosea."

"The land claim around the mine you're talkin' about was first registered to a man named Hosea Povey in 1847."

I blink. "You knew that off the top of your head?"

"Oh yeah." Nick laughs. "Bit of local legend. Ol' Hosea Povey got into a feud with Claiborne Loughton over the land rights *before* it produced any gold. You don't normally see something like that."

"But I thought the Old West had tons of people fighting over land claims... especially when gold's involved."

Nick holds up a finger. "Yes, but things don't get heated until *after* gold is discovered. Hosea worked the land for months and never found even a tiny pellet of gold. It's almost like Claiborne knew the mine would produce a fortune in gold before Hosea did. Anyway, Claiborne being wealthy and all, he had the local law in his pocket. Dispute got to the point ol' Hosea snapped. Completely lost his mind. He up and killed a marshal, a deputy, and his young daughter."

I gasp, my thoughts leaping back to the child's voice I heard screaming when I collapsed outside Vincente's house. "Oh, no... his daughter?"

Dammit! Vincente also mentioned hearing a kid's laughter outside at night. Could there truly be a little girl's spirit stuck there? The scream, I'm sure, had been latent, but giggling isn't often a powerful enough emotion to leave an imprint. I can't explain why a legit innocent wouldn't have moved on. It *has* to be something darker taking advantage of the history.

"Aye. So says the story. No way to know for sure since they never found her body." Nick glances down. "Crying damn shame. Anyway, they hung him for all three murders."

Wow... Hosea. What did you do? "That's so sad."

"Well, there's more to it. As I said, bit of a local legend around here. It's like our regional Jimmy Hoffa story. Keeps changing from year to year. First version's the one I told you already. Man snaps, kills his daughter, then it's either he went on a rampage and killed a US Marshal and a deputy, or shot them when they went to bring him in for the girl's murder. Now, around the time ol' Irwin Loughton took over, someone claimed to find a bunch of letters written by a feller name o' Charles Clapp, with two p's. He claimed on his deathbed to be the one who killed the little girl to drive Hosea mad with grief, on the orders of Claiborne."

I exhale. "Wow. Think it's true?"

"Who can say what drives a man to keep such a secret for so long? The Loughton family had a lot of influence around here back then. Lawmen, judges, pretty much everyone who had any political power, the Loughtons had in their pocket. If Clapp told the truth, it probably took him getting to a point where he didn't care if he lived or died. The Loughton family would have no power over him then. 'Course, you had people saying someone who didn't like the family started the rumor to hurt them once the mining operation took a hard downturn."

"Sounds like a total mess."

"Some of the other stories are even better. I'll spare you the ones about aliens."

Wow. I whistle. "Thanks."

He laughs. "Another legend going around is Hosea worked for Loughton, found gold, and tried to steal it for himself. Resulting shootout killed two lawmen and the girl, who caught a stray bullet inside the house. Yet another story claims Hosea and his daughter picked up and left the area after he decided the mine wouldn't yield much. Went up by Oregon to pan rivers instead, and no one died at all. They think all of it's a fanciful legend."

I shake my head. "Doubtful. Not sure how much credibility you're willing to give a psychic, but Hosea's spirit is definitely haunting the property. He was killed by hanging, and not easy. They didn't do it right. He strangled to death."

"Aye, figured as much. Not the ghost part.

I've seen documents pertaining to his trial and execution. Fairly short affair. Trial only lasted a few hours. Ya know back then, if the whole town says someone did something, especially when you've got two dead lawmen and a dead child, everything's decided before the judge even walks into the courtroom." Nick rubs his chin. "Can see them messin' up the hangin' on purpose if he really did kill a pair of lawmen. Damn awful way to go. They do it to send a message about killing marshals."

"Yeah. Figured as much."

"So you're a real psychic, huh?"

"Yep." I smile.

"What number am I thinking of?"

"The color blue."

He stares—because he tried to trick me. Wasn't thinking of a number at all. "Well, I'll be. Don't s'pose you can hook me up with the lottery numbers?"

I laugh. "Sorry, Mr. Birch. Doesn't work that way. I can't see the future."

He pretends to grumble, then smiles, leaning on the counter. "So, what do you think happened back then?"

"Not entirely sure yet. Only thing I can say with any confidence is Hosea Povey's spirit is not at rest, and he died to a botched hanging. He's also apparently killing anyone who lives in the house by strangulation, or at least affecting their body in a way to simulate strangulation. Vincente told me he's heard a child outside at night, so it's also possible the daughter was really killed."

"Damn shame." Nick looks down.

"Yeah. What kind of man wants gold so bad he's willing to murder a child?"

"A real demon," mutters Nick.

An unusual pang of dread hits me the instant he says 'demon.' Aww, crap.

Sometimes, being a psychic is a real pain. My reaction to the word can only mean there really is a demon involved. Question is: would it be impersonating a little girl or is it lurking somewhere else I haven't looked yet?

Crap. Okay, Universe. I'm on it.

Chapter Six
Botched

I spent most of Monday researching spells and rituals useful for dealing with angry ghosts or demons while Millicent helped.

You'd think since she's a ghost and all, she could fly over there, find the guy, and have a nice chat. Though, if Hosea Povey lost his mind, murdered his daughter, then went on a rampage in which he killed a couple cops... I doubt there'd be anything 'nice' about the chat. So, yeah. It looks like we're dealing with the ghost of a man who died in 1849. He's definitely been a spirit long enough to have learned how to affect the living. There being four people found dead in the house over the years is highly suspicious, even without the corroborating evidence of strangulation in the older cases.

Seriously, what are the odds of every prior owner of a property dying under suspicious circumstances? Edith and Ralph Larsen weren't old enough to spontaneously drop dead of heart attacks... and even if they both had serious health issues, it's unlikely they would've died at the same time. Sure, anything is *possible*. Maybe they committed suicide by pills. Who knows?

At least Monday didn't end up being a total waste of time. We figured out an effective means of attacking spirits using magic. Between my hunches, Millicent's commentary, and a tiny prod from Gaia, I've worked out a new spell to fight ghosts. It's similar to the fireball I've been using, but made entirely out of magic energy. No fire. I haven't tested it yet other than throwing it at empty ground in the alley behind my apartment; however, if my estimations are correct, this spell shouldn't be capable of hurting a living person. Wait. I take that back. It will *hurt* them. People still have souls after all, but I am ninety-nine percent sure this spell can't kill a spirit when it's still inside the body it belongs to. Meaning, if I hit a living person with my 'ghost fireball,' it's probably going to be super painful but not dangerous.

Different story when using it on a specter.

Vincente doesn't call, nor do I experience any random feelings of OMG. Still, I can't help but think about Hosea, his daughter, the two dead cops, and how crazy it must have been back then for a man to reach such a breaking point over land rights, especially land not producing any gold. How sad is it Claiborne ended up taking the mine after they executed Hosea and he found gold right away? Like, if Hosea had spent his time digging instead of killing everyone, he might've been the one to have found the gold. To be *so* close before he gave up, and then have the man who'd been harassing him take the treasure he'd been busting his backside for? Wow. No wonder. Darn good reason for a spirit to be pissed off.

Sometimes, people get far angrier at themselves than anything another person did to them.

I know this whole situation is gnawing on my mind bad since I've referred to three different call-in guests on my Tuesday radio show as 'Hosea' by accident. Fortunately, I'm a psychic, so it's easy to recover from the gaffes by saying a spirit is distracting me. In truth, it's not really a lie. Despite the spirit of Hosea Povey not being right next to me, he's definitely distracting me.

Detective Smithy wants to take me out for

dinner Wednesday or Thursday. Yeah, we're kinda dating. Also, yeah... the queen of 'Hump or Dump' has done a reading on herself and Smithy. How'd he do? Let's just say I'm willing to go on the date. Romance hasn't exactly been kind to me. Most of my hesitation and wanting to take things slow here is coming from fear. However, it's not the usual sort of fear people have in regard to commitment. I'm afraid if we start to get too serious, he's going to get killed on the job. The last time I decided to eject my brain out of my head and fall madly in love with a guy, he ended up dead mere days later.

As soon as I get home from the radio station on Tuesday, I kick my shoes off and head straight to my Spirit Chair. A little distant-seeing session shouldn't take too long. No, I can't explain why the idea to do it didn't happen before work. Sometimes, I don't think of doing stuff when I have ample time. Gotta chalk it up to the Universe sending messages. The strong urge to go snooping around for Hosea's ghost hit me on the ride home.

I'm hopeful it means I'll find something.

After making myself comfortable in the chair, I close my eyes and try to relax. It's not too difficult. Little traffic at this hour, so my commute was pleasant. Most of my anxiety right now is related to Hosea and worry about Vincente's life.

Hosea Povey... I say in my mind-voice, concentrating on a sense of his identity. We— meaning Millicent and I—couldn't find any photographs of the man. All I've got is a name and my memory of feeling the spiritual charge at the property. Psychics with distant-seeing abilities, according to rumor, used to work for the Department of Defense, snooping around at Russian military sites. All they had to go on was a picture taken by a reconnaissance aircraft or satellite and they could find the place. A name, plus what I know of his history, should be plenty.

Hosea Povey... where are you? Who are you? What really happened?

I repeat the name a few times in my mind.

A sense of vertigo comes out of nowhere... as if I've fallen backward out of my body, down through my chair. The feeling is brief, but disconcerting. The darkness of my closed eyelids gives way to weak, flickering firelight illuminating a rough-hewn stone tunnel and a rough rock face straight in front of me. My vision's hazy at the edges, faded to smoky grey. Two lanterns hang above me, one on either side. A man's arms swing into view, hammering a pick axe at the rock.

Again and again, Hosea Povey attacks the wall, chipping away stone. Every so often, he stops, picks up a chunk to examine, then tosses it aside. Frustration, anger, disappointment, and exhaustion saturate his every breath. He's been working here almost two years with nothing to show for it. His wife left him. He can't spend all his time looking for gold because his daughter needs food. Anger, furious anger, wells up... directed at someone *male*.

Everything goes black.

Seconds later, another rush of vertigo makes me feel like I'm falling straight down. Something cinches tight around my throat, excruciatingly painful. Can't breathe. In a panic, I try to grab at my neck, but my arms refuse to move. Horrified gasps come from all around me. Indistinct voices murmur from all directions, some shocked, some angry, some cheering.

My eyes snap open.

I'm in my Spirit Chair, but still can't breathe. Tightness encircles my neck, the texture of a coarse, fat rope crushes my windpipe, pulling so hard it feels like I'm about to go up over the back of the chair. My arms won't move off the armrests. The pressure on my throat is so severe I can't even gasp. Can't move. Can't scream. I'm going to die here. The edges of my vision go black, shrinking into a tunnel. Right as total panic begins to set in, the pressure lets go.

I lurch forward, gasping for air, grabbing my neck, cough-choke-gagging. Bright spots dance in my vision. Severe nausea and light-headedness follow. I flop back in the chair, unable to do anything other than stare at the ceiling and think about how happy I am to simply have the ability to breathe.

As soon as the spots cease dancing in my eyes, I stagger to the bathroom and check myself in the mirror. No red marks. Whew. Okay, honestly, it's not surprising. I didn't feel a ghostly presence in the room with me. Nothing actually choked me out. As real as it felt, I'd essentially read an ancient memory.

Too numb to think, I throw a few handfuls of water in my face, stand there dripping for a moment, then dry off and zombie-shamble to my sofa. Not until I've been staring into space for over ten minutes does the meaning of my experience finally register. Hosea Povey's execution by hanging was definitely botched. He hadn't died instantly, as is supposed to happen. His full weight dangled by his neck as he suffocated over an excruciating few minutes. Even if he murdered his daughter, I can't feel anything but horror at such a death. All those people standing there watching him suffer a slow, agonizing death, no one doing anything to help. His hands would've been tied behind him. No wonder I couldn't move my arms. I shudder merely thinking about the watered-down echo of his experience.

It's quite possible the executioner hadn't made a mistake as much as wanted him to suffer out of revenge for murdering two cops and a child. Justice in the 1800s could be quite brutal, after all. But what happened to fill him with rage to the point he murdered his daughter and two cops? Had he resented her as a burden taking time away from his goal of finding gold? And if he'd been at such a tipping point already, his rival striking gold so soon after his death must have driven his spirit beyond sanity. This is exactly how once-human ghosts turn into paranormal monsters.

That odd feeling of anticipation I first felt at Vincente's house doesn't make any sense.

Only one explanation could possibly account for such a weird emotion in the area—it didn't come from Hosea. He would *definitely* not be happy to see me, or anyone really.

All of a sudden, I have a strong urge to take a closer look at the mine.

Chapter Seven
Second Try

Wednesday. Yay, hump day.

The highlight of my show came from a woman who asked me to check out the man she wanted to make her seventeenth husband. Oddly, neither she nor the guy had any disturbing auras. My best guess is she's the type of person who becomes insanely attached to people (or possessions) real fast, then just as fast, forgets they exist. Didn't sense any malice in her—or the guy—so I took the safest way out. I voted hump, but also told her my psychic hit gave me the feeling they wouldn't last. I suggested they should stay fiancées for a few months before taking it past that point.

Next caller quipped "Number *seventeen*? I'm as psychic as a brick and even I can tell you they won't last."

It's good I've come to really like this job. Even when I can't wait to be done for the day, time *still* flies by. Oh, and the station is doing a gimmicky promotion. Six lucky listeners are going to win an Alcatraz ghost tour sponsored by my show. Sounds fun, right? Only problem is, I've gotta go with them. *So* not looking forward to it. The place is creepy as hell. Adding a genuine psychic to a harsh prison where untold brutality occurred couldn't possibly go wrong in any conceivable way, could it?

Nah. (This is where I bang my head on the desk repeatedly.)

Anyway, after my show, I drive straight to Vincente's place. I called him earlier while on my way to work, asking if it would be okay if I stopped by. He hadn't experienced any further paranormal events other than a few unexplained knocks and his cell phone flinging itself at him. Not sure about the average person, but cell phones flying across the room, to me, counts as more than a minor annoyance.

I get there a few minutes short of 9:00 p.m.

From the instant I open my car door, it's obvious the energy surrounding the house is completely different. It's what I call 'French roast energy': strong, dark, and there's no way anyone's sleeping until it's gone. Vincente meets me at the door. The instant I step into the front room, a soft *thump* emanates from over by the couch.

"Thank you for coming back." He waits for me to finish stepping into the room, then shuts the door.

"Did you hear that?" I point toward the thump.

"Yeah. Phone hit the rug again."

Sure enough, we find his phone on the floor when we walk over there—and it's open to my number in his call history.

"He knows I'm here," I say.

Vincente picks his phone up. "How do you know?"

"Look at the screen. It's showing my number in the recent calls."

He glances down, shrugs. "That's like the tenth time it opened to your contact info. Thought it just glitched."

"Your phone kept showing you my number whenever it went flying?"

"Yeah. Why?"

I exhale. "Oh, wow."

"Is that bad?"

"Hard to say. The ghost is definitely trying

to send some kind of message about me. Considering his history, I'm not too inclined to think he wants me around. It's probably a warning not to invite me back here. Also, crap."

"Crap?" He raises both eyebrows, chuckling.

"Yes. It appears the ghost is still able to get inside the house despite my protection spell. Means he's quite a bit stronger than I thought... or he's not really hostile."

Vincente rubs his throat.

"Oh, would you mind playing the EVP for me again? Any chance the spirit is saying his name is Hosea instead of Jose?"

"Uhh, might be. One moment."

I stand there in the living room while Vincente heads down the hall to grab the digital recorder. Again, a feeling like someone's watching me makes me twist to look into the kitchen. The window over the sink is black as the night outside in the desert, but a definite presence seems to be there. It's not giving off anger, though. Perhaps the spirit of some random miner has come to watch the show—me taking on Hosea.

Vincente returns. He plays the EVP again. It's really damn hard to make out, but if I think about the whispery voice saying 'Hosea' instead of Jose, I can hear it. Ghost voices caught on digital recorders always sound sped up. The 'ay-uh' part at the end of the name is squished to the point it sounds like someone saying 'Jose' with a record skip snap at the end.

"Eh, could be," says Vincente. "Never heard of 'Hosea' as a name."

"It's old. People don't really name their kids that anymore." I share what I learned from Nick, the historian in Kramer Junction, about Hosea Povey being the first non-Native American to live on this land... at least as far as any existing records can claim. "I'm almost certain it's him. The marks I saw on your neck looked like a hangman's rope. They botched—or deliberately screwed up—his execution. He strangled to death over the course of several minutes."

"Ugh." Vincente rubs his throat, grimacing.

A door at the back end of the house slams.

I jump and yelp.

Vincente jumps, too, but doesn't make a sound, giving me side eye. "Why are *you* screaming? Don't you see this stuff all the time?"

"Being around spirits, even expecting one to be here, doesn't make anyone immune from sudden loud noises."

"Guess I've gotten used to them." He winks.

"You still jumped."

He holds his hands up, shaking his head in obviously fake denial.

Our moment of levity doesn't last long before I go serious again. "He is definitely here, and I bet he heard me talking about what they did to him. Even if he did kill his daughter, he didn't deserve—"

Wham!

The entire house shakes.

Ooo-kay. Hosea didn't like that one bit.

I walk to the start of the hallway leading away from the living room. "Hosea? You don't have to keep banging things. You can talk to me the same way you used to talk to people when you were alive."

No reply.

Vincente walks up behind/beside me, staring down the hall.

"Hosea?" I call out.

After another minute of silence, I advance to the first door on the left, the bathroom. No one there, so I poke my head through the door on the right, the smaller bedroom. "Hosea?"

As soon as I back out of the side room, the figure of a man appears in the doorway to the master bedroom at the end of the hall, phasing into existence in mid-stride. The sudden manifestation plus strong aggressive energy makes me jump back, startled, unintentionally leaping into Vincente's arms. Well, more like crashed into him and he grabbed me to keep me from falling over.

Anger falls off the spirit in waves.

For a long, silent few seconds, I lock eyes with the spirit of Hosea Povey.

I'm certain it's him, even though I shouldn't have any way to recognize him. He's much younger than I expected, not far at all into his thirties. The guy's quite muscular, but average in height. Probably tall for his era, though. Brown hair, brown eyes, suntanned. He's no movie star, but I could definitely see him on the cover of a steamy Western novel. And yeah, he looks like a cowboy without a hat, wearing grey pants, a long-sleeved white cotton shirt that looks like the upper half of long johns, and boots.

"What happened?" asks Vincente.

"Sec," I whisper. "Hosea's standing in your bedroom doorway."

He's close to solid-looking, but still transparent enough to be an obvious ghost. Other than a dark red line across his throat, he doesn't have any other obvious signs of injury—such as a broken or stretched-out neck.

Vincente squints, evidently unable to see him at all.

"Hi, Hosea. I'm Allison Lopez. I can see

you. Please talk to me. What can we do to help you rest?"

Hosea keeps staring at me, clenching his fists and relaxing them. I really don't like the look in his eyes, like a bull about to charge. Or a drunk who thinks we said something rude about his little sister.

"Something is keeping you here," I say in a soothing voice. "Spirits aren't supposed to be stuck in this world. I'd like to help you move on. What can you tell me about the marshal—"

Fast as a blur, Hosea rushes at me.

Next thing I know, I'm on my back, a mild dull pain in my chest, and Hosea's attempting to strangle Vincente with an inch-thick rope. Despite the clear rage in his eyes, his facial expression remains calm. It doesn't look like he's truly wrenching down on the spectral rope with any true effort, and I get the weirdest feeling he *isn't* trying to kill. I mean, seriously… throwing a rope around someone's neck and choking them is a pretty strange way to say hello.

Vincente gasps for air, wheezing but not completely unable to breathe. Having no real substance, the ghost clings to him like a backpack, going wherever he staggers. Okay, what the heck? The pain in my chest feels an awful lot like Hosea shoved me out of the way to get at Vincente. I thought for sure he intended to attack me over the protection spell. Making the cell phone keep showing my number had to be a message, right?

Why would he throw me out of the way to get at Vincente?

"Stop!" I yell, while scrambling back to my feet.

The spirit glances at me. At Vincente. Back to me. He seems confused.

"Yes. I can see you."

Hosea loosens the rope. Vincente draws in a huge breath despite the ghost still holding the noose around his neck, evidently without pressure.

"Is he gone?" rasps Vincente.

"Not yet." I raise both hands in a placating manner at the spirit, like a hostage negotiator trying to get the suspect to calm down. Yeah, I watch too much *Law & Order*.

Hosea's anger morphs into frustration and sorrow. Ghosts don't have auras, but I'm getting an unmistakable sense of emotion from him.

"Whoa… hang on." I point at him. "You *didn't* do it, did you?"

The ghost continues staring at me.

I know he's not hung up on being unable to talk due to a strangulation death. If so, he wouldn't have said his name on the digital recorder. "Someone else killed the marshal and the deputy, didn't they?"

Hosea's mood falters back to anger.

"Okay. I can feel you getting mad again. I'll take that as a yes." I step closer to him, reaching out a hand. "Please talk to me. I want to help. Give me a chance to help you. The only thing I ask is you stop hurting people in this house."

He continues staring.

"I spoke to a historian in town. He told me they never found your daughter. What happened?"

Hosea glares, then disappears.

"Crap." I exhale.

"He's gone, isn't he?" Vincente rubs his throat. "It feels different in here all of a sudden. Less heavy."

"Yeah." I collapse against the wall, raking a hand through my hair. "You okay?"

"Fine. Not the worst it's been."

"This is going to sound strange, but I don't think he's trying to kill you."

Vincente tilts his head, giving me the 'are you serious' eyebrow. "What else would he be doing squeezing me so hard I almost pass out?"

"I have an idea, but immediately came up with a counterargument."

"What?" He laughs.

I limply gesture toward the living room. "Your phone kept showing you my number, right? Well, I think Hosea might have been antagonizing the people who live in this house in hopes they would reach out for help to someone like me who can talk to them... but, if he *wanted* someone like me here, why did he disappear instead of speak to me?"

"Huh..." He exhales hard. "Good question. Now what?"

"Now, I'm going to follow up on a hunch I had last night. I think there's possibly another ghost around here, outside. Mind if I take a look?"

"Go right ahead. Want me to come along?"

"I might have better luck alone. Ghosts can be shy."

He folds his arms. "All right. Keep your eyes open for snakes. Do you have a flashlight?"

"Not with me." Darn. It's probably time I replace the batteries in the one I keep in my hall closet, come to think of it. Just my luck, the power will go out and the flashlight will be dead.

Vincente waves for me to follow him. "Let me grab you one."

Chapter Eight
Ragdoll

Exploring the property around an old, abandoned mine isn't the craziest thing I've ever done.

Bear in mind, I have no intention of going *into* the mineshaft. This is me following a hunch, not trying to kill myself. Walking around decaying buildings shouldn't be too dangerous. Admittedly, it is somewhat difficult to tell by flashlight how bad the buildings are. The place had been in operation into the early 1970s, so it's unlikely the 'disturbance' of my footsteps is going to cause a collapse. I mean, they've remained standing *this* long.

I cut across open scrubland to a tall chain

link fence surrounding the property. Not sure I'm going to risk climbing it. Something about the mine is calling to me, but breaking my neck climbing a fence or dying in a cave-in isn't on my top fifty list of stupid things to do. So, I head left along the fence to the corner, planning to squeeze past a gap in the gate if I can find one.

A pair of large fence sections on wheels block off the dirt road leading into the mining company. It appears they *were* secured by padlock and chain... but the lock is open. Confused, I approach with caution, shining my borrowed flashlight through the fence into the yard. Partially rusted trucks stare impassively back at me. None of the inside is paved. Weeds and scrub greenery sprout up everywhere, no different from the land outside the fence. Some grow up out of the wheel wells of abandoned dump trucks. Large buildings as well as a system of overhead conveyors—for loading ore or whatever into open-backed trucks—emit frequent creaks whenever the wind moves.

Okay, maybe walking around in there *is* dangerous. If a bolt or roller falls from one of those elevated belts, it could crush my skull. I might be a witch, but I'm not immortal. Or stupid.

I'm still curious enough to approach the

gate, mostly due to the little bit of shiny silver on the end of the padlock shackle. The part that goes into the housing when the padlock is closed looks pristine, while the rest of it is rusted. I grasp the lock, tilting it upward to check out the keyhole on the bottom. It's entirely blocked by rust. King Kong wouldn't be strong enough to force a key into there.

"This is not normal." I let the lock fall against the gate, clattering metal.

Someone or something opened this recently. Of course, I'm no expert on breaking and entering. It's possible some teenagers crowbarred it open. I shine the flashlight on the ground inside the gate, searching for the footprints of whoever popped the gate... but the dirt is undisturbed. Hmm. So, someone randomly wandered by a mine out here in the middle of nowhere, broke open the padlock, and left.

Makes total sense... not.

Another creak comes from the big overhead conveyor mechanism crossing the open gap between buildings down the main 'street' into the mine. Each one of the rollers in it has to be as big as an entire deli bologna log. Still, the itch to go inside is pulling me stronger than my fear. On the upside, if one of those rollers falls and nails me in the head, I won't feel a damn thing.

I'd just be dead.

So, yeah. Stupid me... I ease the left gate section aside and squeeze past the gap. This yard is eerily quiet—creaking metal aside—to the point the rattling chain link sounds like a thunderclap. I half expect police to show up any second. Feels like I'm in some kind of post-apocalyptic scenario or even a *Silent Hill* movie.

Moving forward, I'm soon surrounded on all sides by empty buildings. Probably used to be offices or even bunk houses. The conveyor system connects to the second stories of what appears to be two giant storage warehouses. Another building where most of one wall has collapsed contains all sorts of huge machinery. I don't know the first thing about mining, but my guess is the big machines are related to ore processing.

Near the midway point of the property, I walk past the corner of the larger warehouse, which allows me to see the mine entrance itself in the hills at the back of the compound. Boards and planks attempt to block it off, with 'danger' signs plastered all over. Looks like someone broke in already, pulling away a board or three to create a hole big enough for someone to crawl through.

Yeah, so... if 'death' had a picture in the

dictionary, it would be this mine entrance.

I'm honestly surprised looking at it doesn't give me any terrifying psychic premonitions of my imminent demise. Oh, right. I'm not getting any of those because I'm not going in there. Period.

Hmm. No idea what to do now. None of these buildings look remotely safe to touch, much less explore. I turn in place, shining the flashlight around at windows, doorways, and an alley between the office building and warehouse two.

"What the heck made me want to check this place out?"

When I swing the flashlight back over the mine entrance, a flash of white catches my eye. What the hell? Despite knowing I'll regret it, I point the light at the mine again.

A little blonde girl is standing in front of the barrier, staring expectantly at me.

She's maybe ten, barefoot, and dirty like one of those kids you see in photographs from the Great Depression. Her white dress is old-fashioned, but plain to the point she could be from the 1920s as easily as the mid-1800s. An equally simple ragdoll dangles from her left hand at her side. The instant I see her, a spike of sadness stabs me in the heart.

The child is partially transparent. Dark

spots, gaps between boards closing off the mine, are visible through her body. Only the strange mood coming from her stops me from crying. This kid is the source of the unusual anticipation in the air around Vincente's property. I suppose her being a child explains why the mood reminds me of a kid on Christmas morning waiting for their grandparents to show up.

Something clicks in my brain.

"Oh, wow... Hosea didn't keep making the phone show my number. You did."

She smiles.

Legitimate child ghosts are rare. Demons and other dark creatures routinely pretend to be little kids to mess with the living. Ever notice how so many supposedly haunted areas always have stories of little kids running around? Admittedly, I can't claim to have been seeing ghosts for a long time, but this is the first kid spirit I've seen, and she's not setting off any alarm bells in my mind.

"Hosea is your father?"

She nods.

As soon as I start approaching, she smiles again and darts into the mine tunnel, waving for me to follow. Ah, hell no. Her spectral form ignores the wooden barrier as if it didn't exist. She collapses into a shimmering orb of glowing light that zooms into the darkness out of sight.

Dammit.

I told myself not to go in there. Why does it now feel like something I *have* to do?

This has more than 'bad idea' written on it. Try giant glowing neon letters spelling out 'death' over the opening. Metaphorically, of course. Psychics talk about seeing signs everywhere, but it's not literal. Still, I'm not picking up any sense of ominous dread upon giving serious consideration to following the ghost.

C'mon, Allie. I got into a fight with a massive Jaguar earthquake god. I can handle a tunnel.

Before I can think too much about it, emotion wins out over reason. I hurry past a line of old dump trucks and a cluster of mine carts. A few railroad ties in the ground follow the path of a former train track into the depths. Pretty sure they tore those tracks up once wheeled vehicles became a thing. Actual mine carts most likely hadn't been used here since the Forties. Someone probably salvaged the rails for metal but left the wood. Jaw clenched, I drop to my hands and knees, peering through the opening in the barricade. Dust and the dry scent of earth fills my senses, along with a fleeting hint of flowers. The pleasant aroma is gone so fast it can't have possibly come from anything real.

The flashlight illuminates a rock-walled tunnel, more wooden railroad ties, and an assortment of old crates, tools, and other junk left behind by the mining company when they shut the site down. Seems open enough. This section of tunnel is wide enough to drive a full-sized car into.

White light appears maybe fifty feet ahead in the dark, growing out from a baseball-sized orb into the same little girl. She gives me a look like 'what are you waiting for?' No psychic warning sirens ring out, so I do the dumbest thing I can think of… and crawl past the barrier into the shaft.

She watches patiently while I stand and swat dust off my knees.

"What is it you want me to see?" I ask.

The child runs off down the tunnel.

A sense of gloom surrounds me, but not in a manner that feels like a warning. Something horrible happened here. Considering I am following a young girl's ghost, it's fairly obvious what awful act left such an imprint on the area.

"Wait… why are you running off?"

She keeps going.

My voice echoes back to me a few times.

I cautiously follow her deeper into the mine, keeping my flashlight trained on the ground to watch out for hazards. Can't tell if the faint, distant clanking of people digging is coming from my imagination or the restless spirits of miners who died here. The sound is so quiet it could easily be all in my head. Or I'm picking up another imprint left on the tunnel.

The kid darts left, vanishing into a side passage.

"Wait!" I call out.

Dammit.

There could be holes, animals, bugs, snakes, low-hanging spiders, who knows what lurking in the dark. As much as I'm driven to pursue this ghost to see what she's so desperate to show me, I can't bring myself to move any faster than a careful creeping walk. Fortunately, she didn't go *too* far. The left-branching tunnel is surprisingly close to the mine entrance... and it's tiny, clearly dug out by hand—meaning not modern power tools.

I cringe, shining the flashlight around the edges of an opening about the size of a submarine door... or maybe a little bit larger. It's roughhewn, unlike the large tunnel I'm standing in. Crude wooden braces at roughly ten-foot intervals struggle to hold up the earth overhead, some visibly cracked and bowing under the weight bearing down on them. Ah, hell. I take a moment to remind myself a tunnel is nowhere near as scary as a giant ancient god. How can I prove this? Simple. The average person wouldn't enjoy going down this tunnel, but doing so wouldn't put them in a mental institution for the rest of their lives. Most people seeing a moving god-statue big enough to grab people like Barbie dolls would at least end up on a therapist's couch if not in a padded room. Wait, no. Not quite accurate. A Barbie doll to a human is bigger than we were to the Jaguar god's stone avatar.

Deep breath. The Universe wants me here. I know it without a shadow of a doubt.

Gaia has my back. I hope.

I creep down the narrow passageway. Seven crumbling wooden braces later I reach a split where the tunnel breaks off into three different directions. The ghost appears again in the distance, straight in front of me.

"Hey, sweetie. You don't have to run away from me."

She darts off into the dark.

Grr.

Yeah, I get she's trying to lead me to something, but why can't she walk with me? Don't understand the weird cat-and-mouse thing ghosts do. Grumbling mentally, I keep going straight at the three-way fork, continuing to make my way deeper into the earth. An extremely stressed wooden brace forces me to duck under it. It has to be quite old, since it appears to be round like a tree trunk, not a square beam. Even at a foot thick, the wood's bent to the point it's cracked on the bottom.

I ease myself past the dagger-like splinter jutting down from the midpoint, whispering a protection chant. Sometimes, I'm *really* jealous of Sam's ability to teleport. So damn handy. However, I'm not willing to die to get it. Besides, teleportation isn't a guarantee. According to her, it's a fairly rare ability even among vampires. She thinks it has something to do with her ancestry… so maybe, being a witch, I *would* be so lucky. Meh. Not worth it. Even though I won't remember any of my past lives, the idea of no longer being able to reincarnate bothers me. The sense of loss I feel at Sam being separated from the trifecta the three of us shared for centuries will forever keep me unwilling to pursue immortality. I'd rather our souls share the continuing bond, even if my immediate memories of lifetimes reset every sixty to ninety years.

"C'mon, kiddo. Don't run off. I want to help."

The girl reappears abruptly right in front of me. "So do I."

"Gah!" I jump back, fumbling the flashlight.

It hits the dirt between my feet, shining back the way I came. For a few seconds, I can't do anything but clamp both hands over my heart and try to remember how to breathe.

Unfazed by my brief scream, the little girl looks up at me. She's giving off enough light to remain clearly visible and even illuminate the walls around her... about as bright as one of those chemical glow sticks. Inches behind her heels, the tunnel floor drops off.

"Holy crap! I almost walked straight off a cliff."

"Yes." She twists innocently side to side.

Once I recover from the shock of her sudden appearance, I say, "Thank you."

She nods. The girl's odd calm breaks to a desperate, pleading stare. "Please help us. Papa didn't do this." She points at the shaft behind her and disappears, making everything in front of me dark again.

"Wait..."

Sigh.

I crouch to pick up the flashlight, keeping one hand on the wall for balance. Still squatting, I point the light forward. The tunnel ends at a vertical shaft. Against my better judgment, I take one step closer, lean forward, and point the light down. Old wood beams hang from the walls here and there, with a giant pile of them at the bottom. They appear to be the remains of a primitive elevator, little more than a platform and pulleys one person could use to pull themselves up. Of course, it's all broken, the ropes long-ago rotted.

This shouldn't scare me at all considering I've ridden on the back of Sam's dragon form. As best I can recall, we flew at like 1,500 feet off the ground. No way is this hole deeper than that. Still, my lack of fear came from a specific source: magic. Falling from 1,500 feet doesn't take too long to hit the ground, but it's still enough time for me to cast a quick spell. A thirty- or forty-foot fall in a mine can kill easily, and not give me the chance to cast a spell before I break my neck.

Easy answer for that, though. I enchant myself with my 'parachute' spell *before* falling. It essentially reduces my weight to about a pound or two. If I'd fallen off Talos, I'd have drifted to the ground gently enough to survive and probably not even suffer serious injury. Yeah, I've got a strong feeling the girl wants me to see something at the bottom of this shaft.

I sigh and study the shaft.

As much as I can see with the flashlight, rough rock walls surround a drop of about sixty feet or more to a tangled pile of old lumber. This is probably a dumb idea, but I'm fairly sure I can get out of here. The same 'parachute' spell also makes it easier to climb things since I'm temporarily light. Hey, who needs physics when I have magic, right?

Dammit. This kid wants me to see something down there, right?

Okay, deep breaths. You got this, Allie.

Still, two random emotions hit me at once. A sense of reassurance, which has to be coming from Gaia… and a need to do this now, which is either my witchy premonition or simply me being a sucker for a kid in need of help. Yeah, sure, she *might* be a demon trying to lure me down there before causing a cave-in. But, if so, Gaia *wouldn't* have given me a 'go on, child, it's okay' mental back-pat.

There's a web comic where a heart and brain constantly get into arguments. A similar scenario is going on inside me at the moment. Heart wants to go down. Brain is yelling, 'Nope. Nope. Nope.' Screw it. Heart wins.

Vincente's flashlight has a belt clip, so I attach it to the waistband of my jeans, leaving it on and pointed down, then gingerly lower myself over the edge. There's no ladder or anything here to grab onto for climbing other than the rock walls and what remains of the old elevator beams. Even with magic keeping me light, I'm afraid to touch the rickety wooden structure.

Foot by foot, I lower myself, trying not to pay attention to how far I'm going. At least it's so damn dark above me, I can't see the top. Makes it less scary because I can pretend it's only a short distance.

I bump some wood, knocking it loose... and it falls. The *thud* echoes up a disturbingly long time later. Since I'm not really afraid of falling, I break the cardinal rule and look down. A faint glow from the little spirit seems to be another four stories below. Wow. Did Hosea dig this vertical shaft all by himself in two years, or did he find an already-dug mine and decide to keep working in it? The guy from the historical society told me Hosea acquired this land in 1847. This seems like an awful deep hole to dig in a mere two years with a pickaxe. At least some of this has to be a natural cavern.

Oh, to hell with it.

I let go and allow myself to glide to the bottom.

Naturally, the girl's gone when I land.

"Okay, what did you want me to see?" I ask... to no response.

After waiting another minute or five, I crouch and scan the flashlight over the debris collected at the bottom of the shaft, mostly loose dirt that's fallen from the walls over the years. A short tunnel leads away from the bottom, going barely six feet before it stops at a rounded end. The pickaxe used to excavate the small offshoot is still leaning against the wall, suggesting he hadn't been done going deeper here. An inexplicable notion tells me this is the last spot Hosea worked in the mine before he died. Strange, though… not getting any dark energies here. Unless there's a weird fungus or something in the air potentially responsible for his mental state.

Boy, what if he really *didn't* kill anyone?

I continue rummaging around the scrap wood from the old elevator. A dingy lump of cloth sticks up out of the dirt beside a large pulley box. Shining the flashlight directly at it reveals the head of a rag doll. Small human bones litter the area around it.

My heart sinks.

A distant child's scream echoes from above me. She fell? The girl said her papa didn't do it. Maybe she tried to find him after he shot the marshal and slipped. No wonder they never found her body. Even back in 1849 when this elevator thing was intact, I don't think many people would have been willing to hop on it and come down here.

My flashlight beam reveals a half-buried skull about the right size for a ten-year-old. The entire left side of the cranium is smashed open. The instant I see it, I know the girl died from falling into this hole.

Something compels me to unearth the ragdoll. I pluck it out of the ground, gently shaking it to knock loose dirt away. As soon as I hold it up, such sorrow overwhelms me, I lose my composure and end up sobbing, clinging to the ragdoll as if it were mine.

Chapter Nine
Not Time

"Don't cry," whispers a childish voice.

I look up at the glowing apparition of Hosea's daughter. She's standing beside me, one hand on my shoulder, making a face like a little girl playing mother to one of her dolls. Her cornflower-blue eyes glimmer with hope and happiness. The disconnect between such a tragic death and this spirit being *happy* short-circuits my brain. My tears stop in an instant.

"I'm Allison," I rasp past the lump in my throat.

Up close, it's obvious her dress is older than I initially thought. Definitely from the 1800s. It's filthy, threadbare, and patched in spots, probably the only dress she had. Wild blonde hair hangs a little past her waist, giving her something of a feral look. It's a little difficult to tell due to her bluish-white glow, but she has a bit of a suntan. Dirt outlines her fingernails and toenails. She doesn't look as if they had much money at all. Poor kid's kinda thin, too. Guessing she didn't eat well.

"You can help us. I know you can." The girl smiles. "I'm Dorothea."

"Hi, Dorothea. Are you a real spirit or something else trying to trick me?"

She tilts her head. "I don't know what you mean."

The urge to hug her is strong, but futile, so I resist. "Children your age don't usually end up as ghosts."

"Oh." She smiles. "I didn't go to Heaven because the angel said it's not time for me yet. I wasn't supposed to die when I did. A demon killed me."

Say what? I blink. "A demon?"

Dorothea points.

I aim the flashlight at the spot. A knot of frayed rope lays among the bones, tied in such a way as to suggest someone bound her hands before throwing her down here. "Oh, no…"

"Everyone thinks Papa hurt me, but he didn't. Two bad men came to the house. They said Papa had been hurt and I needed to go with them. They tied me up and threw me in here. I don't really remember it. I was so scared, I fainted before they threw me."

"Oh, Dorothea…"

"It's okay. I knew you would find me. You can make it better because demons shouldn't be here. Miss Betty will help you find me." Dorothea hugs me—with all the solidity of a breeze—and disappears.

Wait, what? I wipe tears on the back of my arm. Is Dorothea trapped here as a ghost because the world thinks her father killed her? I'm assuming 'Miss Betty' is the name of this ragdoll. If showing it to people as proof of finding her remains is what she wants me to do, I've got my work cut out for me. Who the heck am I supposed to show this to? Maybe Nick at the Kramer Historical Society. Is he going to believe me? This ragdoll could have come from anywhere.

Great. I'm like a hundred feet down a hole in a dangerous, abandoned mine. Now what?

I sigh upward at the darkness. I'm too emotionally burned out to think about anything right now. Do I leave her remains here as a grave or gather them for a proper burial? Technically, she's already buried… a wee bit deeper than six feet under. I'm not equipped to carry bones. Her remains are so old, the skeleton has fallen apart. It would take me hours to sift the dirt and collect every bit, and I can't stuff her in my jean pockets. For now, she has to wait here. I'll come back with a bag as soon as I can.

The supernatural feeling making me want to check out the mine is gone, leaving me stuck with the realization I'm in a literal deathtrap and absolutely *do not* want to be here. After casting my parachute spell again to make myself lighter, I begin the long climb. Hauling myself up is fairly easy when my body weight is about two pounds. I'm not worried about the climb itself, but the ceiling coming down on me.

Please, tunnel, don't cave in now.

Chapter Ten
Focus Issues

Vincente had been shocked to see me covered in dirt.

Naturally, he kinda flipped out a little when I told him about going into the mine. It took me a while to convince him it hadn't been my intent, and only a magical pull from Gaia gave me the confidence to follow the ghost girl within. Bringing the ragdoll into the house also quieted Hosea's spirit, who'd been knocking stuff around in the master bedroom.

Saying, "I know you didn't hurt Dorothea" didn't convince Hosea to show himself or talk to me... but for the hour or so Vincente and I spoke after, no poltergeist-type activity occurred in the house. It didn't quite feel like he'd gone away for good, but he definitely appeared to be calmed. The whole ride home, my head spun with possible explanations for what might have happened 170 years ago.

Dorothea didn't accidentally fall down a shaft and die while searching for her father. For some reason, two men abducted and killed her. Maybe not 'some reason.' She told me a demon killed her. Also, her father and that Claiborne guy had been feuding over the property rights to the mine. Maybe the rich guy hired two men to get rid of Hosea, they couldn't find him, and took their frustrations out on her instead.

Or they wanted to be cruel.

Could the men who killed Dorothea have been the marshal and the deputy that Hosea Povey supposedly killed? Claiborne supposedly had the whole town in his pocket. Hosea certainly had a motive based on revenge for his daughter's killing. But according to the historian, everyone believed he'd killed her. Considering the amount of influence Claiborne had, it's more than plausible to consider him responsible for hiring a pair of thugs then pinning the death on Hosea to get him out of the way. But if so, wouldn't there have been *some* records of bribery? Stuff like that never stays hidden forever. Hmm. Perhaps not if the authorities of the time covered it up. As they say, history is written by the victor—or the powerful.

Claiborne bribes the local law into helping him get Hosea off the land so he can take the mine...

Two dirty cops kill Hosea's daughter.

Hosea hunts them down for revenge, then gets labeled a murderer, even blamed for murdering Dorothea, too.

Gah. I hope I'm wrong. Something like that would make for one heck of an angry haunt.

My thinking circles back to what the girl said about demons as I park outside my apartment. It's a little after one in the morning, so not only am I emotionally exhausted from the grief of finding Dorothea's remains, I'm physically tired as well. At least there's no need for me to wake up early. Staying up until one or two in the morning isn't as big a deal anymore.

I go inside, set the ragdoll on the kitchen counter next to my purse for now, then head to the bathroom for a shower. There have been times in the past where I've considered myself dirty, but none of them hold a candle to the level of dirt involved with crawling around an abandoned mine shaft. I'm so filthy I almost don't want to put my clothes in the hamper because they'll make the other dirty clothes even dirtier. Yeah, I know. Silly.

While watching brown water roll down my body, over my toes, and disappear into the drain, I try to think about how demons might be involved. Dorothea said an angel told her she hadn't been supposed to die yet. Based on multiple conversations with Sam, I've come to understand each reincarnated life lasts as long as it takes for the soul to learn whatever lesson or accomplish whatever goal is set before it for a given lifetime. Like when her son Anthony almost died as a little boy, he'd done everything he needed to do in this lifetime. Still not sure what the heck a little kid can 'accomplish' in such a short time. Sam agreed with me. She wasn't about to let the universe steal her son from her, so she threw a giant cosmic monkey wrench into the gears.

Something unbelievable is going on with the boy. Feels weird even calling Anthony a boy anymore, he's so tall. He'd been giving off some strange energy… powerful and warm. It's so stupid, but being around him always makes me feel safe, even though he's less than half my age. No, I'm not a big wimp. The kid seriously sends out protective vibes. And now I know why…

The Universe has big plans for Anthony— angelic plans. But that's another story…

Anyway, I'm going off on a tangent here.

Shampoo-massaging my scalp sends another wave of dirt down my body, but also jogs my brain. Dorothea's comment about the angel telling her she hadn't been supposed to die yet must mean her soul didn't accomplish its goal this time around. Not sure how that translates to her lingering as a ghost instead of going into the glowing tunnel and simply hopping on the merry go round again as a new person. But... for whatever reason, here she is. Or there she was, technically, since she didn't follow me home.

This gets me wondering if a demon interfering with a soul's journey opens the possibility for further rule-bending. Also makes me wonder why her guardian angel didn't step in if demons aren't 'allowed' to interfere with mortals who don't invite them. Thinking about her being a legitimate child ghost gets me crying in the shower all over again.

I can't help but think how terrifying it must have been for her. Did she know the men intended to drop her down a shaft to her death? Or did she think they brought her into the mine to hide her? No, the fear I felt when I hit my head on my car had been way too intense. She totally knew what they planned to do to her.

Grr. Bad thoughts. I'll stand here in the shower all damn night if I don't break away from this morbid train of thought.

When the water running off me finally stops looking like weak coffee, I rinse off one more time, shut the water off, and pull the sliding glass shower door open—to find Millicent standing there. She's not *trying* to scare me, but I still jump a little. Getting used to it, at least. Didn't scream.

"I don't believe the purpose of the ragdoll is to prove Hosea didn't kill her," says Millicent.

"Oh?" I step out of the tub and grab a towel.

Millicent turns, continuing to face me. "Discovering the location of her remains doesn't prove or disprove the *who* of her murder."

"There's rope. Her father wouldn't have needed to tie her up. He'd have tricked her."

"Who exactly are you going to convince? The historian?"

I sigh. "What else am I supposed to do with it?" I wrap my head in the towel, hiding from the world. "I saw her skull, Millie. Crushed open."

"You are more upset over what happened to Dorothea than she is."

"How am I supposed to feel about a little girl being murdered?"

Millicent makes a sympathetic sound. "Oh, I suppose exactly as you are feeling. But don't ignore the child's optimistic demeanor. There must be some reason for it."

I pull the towel down off my face, staring through a curtain of hair at my ghostly room-mate. "I'm sure there is. She wanted me to take the doll. Said it's going to help me."

"Yes. I believe she is correct."

"How?"

"How do I believe she is correct or how is it going to help you?"

I smirk. "Second one. No point questioning you on why you think anything."

"Ahh, so you've finally learned." She winks. "Use the doll as a focus item when meditating in the Spirit Chair. I also suggest you hold the Mount Shasta crystal to boost your power as much as possible."

Hmm. Not a bad idea. "Okay, but I'm beat. I'll do it tomorrow."

Millicent folds her arms, giving me a Mona Lisa smile.

By the time I've finished drying off, my guilt and sadness over Dorothea's fate gets the better of me.

I sigh. "Okay, fine."

Chapter Eleven
Guardian Angel

My bathrobe is comfy.

Not sure if it's due to laziness or being in a rush, but I almost meditated wearing a wet towel. My bathrobe happened to be hanging on the hook on the back side of the bathroom door, right there in front of me. Considering I didn't bother tying the belt closed, I'm going to chalk it up to laziness.

Yeah, I'm tired.

Maybe it will work to my advantage. It's sometimes easier to slip into an altered state of consciousness when exhausted. The line between dreams and magical visions is often extremely thin. Some occultists *can't* get visions unless they dream. According to Milli-cent, certain mystical traditions—most of which died out centuries ago—had perfected the art of 'dream magic' to the point they could invade other people's dreams and even kill them. Or create dream ghosts, manifesting in reality far away from their physical location. The story she told me involved an assassin from what's now called Iran falling into a dream trance and creating an apparition of himself halfway across the world to kill someone who'd wronged their sect. Contract killing without ever physically leaving his bedroom.

Wild.

Part of me is glad the art died out.

Anyway…

I relax in my Spirit Chair, holding Doro-thea's ragdoll in one hand, my Mount Shasta crystal in the other. After going through my calming and focusing steps, I open my magical awareness to the universe, focusing it into the doll in a manner similar to using binoculars to see far away. What did Dorothea mean the doll could help? What happened? What does the Universe want me to do here? Why did I feel an intense desire to involve myself with Vincente's situation as soon as I heard his voice?

These thoughts swirl around my head again and again while I strain to see into the blackness of my closed eyes, trying to pry a vision out of the depths of the universe.

The crystal in my right hand heats up slightly.

My body goes weightless.

Whoa. What the heck?

Before the sensation of being a helium balloon fully registers, I abruptly plummet over backward. It's as if my Spirit Chair evaporated, allowing me to fall straight down. Only, I go right through the floor, too, continuing to fall into some kind of void. Blackness surrounds me. I can't even open my mouth to scream.

Oh, God. Please don't be a first-person view of Dorothea's murder. Please tell me I'm not falling down the mineshaft vicariously.

I hit the ground on my back, way softer than seems appropriate for the speed of my fall. As the chaos of the abrupt descent fades, I become aware of lying on dirt under a hot sun. My throat hurts like I've been screaming, though I haven't made a sound. A dry breeze blows across my face. I open my eyes to the desert, late in the afternoon. As soon as I try to raise an arm to shield myself from the glare, it becomes apparent my hands are tied behind my back. The instant I realize I'm bound, my wrists and ankles burn with soreness. I peer down at myself. The dingy child's dress, lack of womanly shape, and dirty bare feet tell me I'm seeing out of Dorothea's eyes. I can't straighten my legs out due to being hogtied.

Hunger and fear claw at me.

Two men stand about ten paces away, openly discussing how they're going to kill me. Both kinda look like Wild West gunslingers who've fallen on hard times, their clothes dirty and worn. The reek of whiskey and body odor is overpowering, even from a distance. The older of the two, who's probably in his early thirties, has short black hair and totally looks like the second fiddle bad guy from a cheesy Western movie. His companion, almost a decade younger, is wearing six-shooters, but looks more like the 'farmer who picked up pa's guns after they lost the farm'.

A small one-room shack not far behind them on my right feels like it's Hosea's place. Looks hand-built. It's a little hard to say, but the hills in the distance are familiar, the same ones behind Vincente's house.

Black Bart—for lack of a better name—jabs a hand at his accomplice in time with his words. "I say we just cut her and be done with it. Let her bleed out."

"You lost yer mind, Charles?" asks the other guy. "Won't anyone be believin' it that way Let's stick to the original plan."

Okay, this is really weird. Usually, when I get a vision, it doesn't feel quite so much like I'm actually here, experiencing the past. Things tend to play out in front of me as though I'm watching a movie. Sure, *sometimes*—especially when using an item like the ragdoll with a strong emotional connection—I see from the point of view of whoever made the emotional imprint. However, this is different, new, and way freaky. Normally, all I can do is watch. But… I'm moving. Like, if I want to squirm or wiggle a finger, it's happening as *I* want it to.

Visions aren't supposed to do that.

Why can't I move? asks Dorothea's voice in my head.

Huh, what?

I'm hearing voices. Papa! Help!

Shh…

"Micah, you ain't thinkin' about this the right way," says Charles. "The more horrible the scene, the more the town's gonna call for his head."

The younger killer shakes his head hard, his long, unkempt brown hair swishing back and forth. "Nah. We wait for dark."

Charles points at Micah's face. "You quit bein' a chicken. Talkin' like ya don't have the stomach for it."

"Yeah, so what. It's a little girl. Ain't her

fault. Don't gotta be nasty 'bout it. Ain't no reason she suffers."

"All the more reason." Charles turns his head to stare at me. The instant we lock eyes, I know for a fact he's possessed—his eyes are solid black. "The younger they are, the more I love the screams."

Considering Micah isn't reacting at all to such a freakishly evil apparition, I'm going to assume he can't see the black eyes.

Dorothea shrieks in my mind. Being inside her head, I know she'd been struggling frantically to free herself for at least ten minutes before my arrival, listening to the men discuss the exact means by which they would kill her. Being paralyzed due to my presence is *really* freaking her out.

Shh… Dorothea, it's going to be okay. I'm here to help. Think of me as a good spirit.

Am I really saying that? Do I really believe this is more than a simple vision of the past?

They're going to hurt me! I didn't do anything. Why do they want to kill me?

Because they're bad. Grr. I don't care if this is real or a dream… I am *not* going to let them hurt an innocent child.

"Not happening. We do this my way or not at all." Micah fidgets. "Can't shoot her on account o' someone hearin' the shots. They gotta think she's been dead afore them lawmen."

"You are a fool, ya know that, Micah?" Charles spits to the side. "I know damn well they'd hear a gunshot from here. Knife takes longer. Hang 'er up like a deer. Let her bleed out slow."

No! screams Dorothea, desperate to free herself, but she can't presently control her body.

Micah blanches. "Uhh, okay, what about this? You don't wanna be here all damn day. Let's take her into the mine. Drop her down a deep shaft, break her neck or something. Be over quick."

Dorothea starts freaking out.

Don't panic, sweetie. They're not going to hurt you. Not with me here.

Hearing her whimper is making me furious.

I roll over onto my right side so my hands aren't squished into the dirt under me. Both men laugh at me 'struggling to escape.' Only a truly sick pair of bastards would openly talk about murdering a child right in front of her. I'm sure the damn demon possessing Charles is adoring every minute of the torment such a conversation is having on her.

With my—well, Dorothea's—hands no longer trapped between her back and the ground, I can conjure a small knife. Well, I hope to! I have no idea if I can perform magic in another's body. Mostly since I've never tried.

Conjuration comes in really handy sometimes... like when I made myself a motorcycle helmet for the ride on Talos. No, the helmet wasn't to save me in case I fell. Not only would it have done nothing to save me from a 1,500-foot fall, I had the spell to slow me down. No, the helmet was for wind. Try flying 300 MPH on the back of a dragon without a helmet and see how fun it is.

One nice thing about conjured knives. I can make them as sharp as physically possible—like lightly serrated obsidian. A second after wanting it to happen, I'm relieved to discover a four-inch dagger has materialized in my hand.

Wow! Where did you get a knife from?

I made it.

Like a magic trick?

Like magic. No trick. It's not real... it's going to disappear in like an hour.

While Micah works on convincing Charles to murder Dorothea/me by throwing us headfirst down the mineshaft, I cut at the ropes binding my wrists. The little razor-sharp knife shreds the ropes like I'm cutting marshmallows. Neither man notices me get my hands loose.

I still have three big problems. First: my ankles are tied together. The men will see me start cutting the rope. No way will they just stand there letting me do it. As soon as my hands come out from behind my back, they're going to jump on me. Second problem: I have two men here who want to kill me—Dorothea. Third issue: I don't want to kill people in front of a child. Even if I've somehow hijacked her body, she's still watching. Hmm. Charles is possessed by a demon. No wonder the angel said her death didn't count. It hadn't been an act of mortals.

Time to test out my new spell.

I sit up, fling my arms forward, and cast the 'ghost killing' spell. The guys spin toward me as a spectral fireball flies from my right hand, cruising at the speed of a fastball into Charles. It hits him dead center in the chest, knocking him back in a stagger. He screams as if stung by 500 bees all at once, throws his head back, and vomits a geyser of dark black liquid.

Micah blinks at the sight of the fireball, clearly not believing his eyes. At the eruption of demonic slime, he forgets entirely about me sitting there and gawks at Charles. Perfect. I cast an entrancement spell on him, knocking him out under a charm of magical sleep. Both men collapse to the ground at the same time. Black vapor swirls up from Charles, beginning to form into a humanoid shape.

I throw another 'ghost fireball' at the mass

of darkness. The white-glowing bolt of magical energy disappears into the inky cloud. A brief flicker of light precedes the vaporous horror exploding, setting off a low, rumbling thunder-clap that seems to roll out to the horizon. Oh, wow. Pretty weak for a demon. Must have been a minor underling. Hopefully, I won't have to worry about the bigger demon responsible for bringing it here. It's also possible Charles had some issues bad enough to attract a random demonic attachment. So, yeah. Might not be a 'bigger demon' around here.

Both men appear to be unconscious.

Demon? whispers Dorothea. *Wow, are you a magician?*

Not exactly. I'm a witch, but don't be scared. I'm an earth witch. Think faeries and nature and life energy. Not evil.

Witches are real?

Yes. And just like people, some are good, some are bad, but most are just kinda there.

Those men wanted to hurt me. What do we do now?

I sit up, saw the rope off my ankles, and grab the ragdoll up from the ground.

"Now? We run."

Chapter Twelve
A Vision Most Unusual

Bizarre doesn't even begin to describe this situation.

Divination, scrying, crystal-ball gazing, reading tea leaves… whatever you want to call it, I've done it countless times in my life. Never before have I managed to end up being able to actively control what goes on. For all intents and purposes, I've become Dorothea. Her body is mine for the time being while her consciousness has receded to a voice in the back of my head. If Millicent and I had written a list of the top 5,000 things to do while scrying someone, possessing them wouldn't be on it. I didn't think it even possible.

Yet, here I am.

For a half-starved, terrified ten-year-old, Dorothea is—

I'm eleven.

Sorry. You're kinda small for your age. Okay, for a half-starved eleven-year-old, she can run pretty darn fast. It's been a few years since I was a child. Forgot what it felt like to have boundless energy.

Don't go home! They'll find me there.

Wasn't planning to. Umm… those guys want people to think your father hurt you. Best thing we can do is be *seen.* Crap. Which way is it to Kramer Junction?

I don't know. There isn't a town named that here. Just Augustown.

Augustown? Never heard of it. Whatever. Can't be picky right now. We need to go somewhere people can see you. There's nowhere to hide out here in the desert. And going to the mine is a really bad idea. So is your house.

Umm. That way.

Which way?

I can't point. My arms don't work.

Sorry. I don't know why this happened.

It's okay. You saved me. I don't want to die. She sniffles mentally. *Turn right a little.*

Just think about the way to go. I can see your thoughts.

She does. I head in the direction she wants to go, running as fast as her legs can carry us.

Despite being a child, we eventually run out of steam and can't sprint anymore. At least Hosea's little house is so far away behind me it's out of sight. My sleep spell should keep Micah out cold for at least an hour. No idea how long Charles is going to be out, though. I've never blasted a demon out of someone before. Considering he'd been possessed, I have mixed feelings about him potentially dying. Not sure how much of his intent to kill Dorothea came from the demon. Then again, Micah didn't have a demonic hitchhiker and he still wanted to hurt this child. It's probably a safe assumption to conclude neither one of those men were 'fine upstanding citizens.'

Still. Don't want to kill them with a child watching.

I'm sure they deserved it, but it is wrong to kill.

You're right.

Why did they want to hurt me?

I'm still trying to figure it out. I stagger to a halt, out of breath, stooped forward. Can't stand still too long since the dirt's kinda hot and Dorothea doesn't have any shoes on.

They don't fit me anymore. Papa can't afford to buy new ones. All that's gonna change once he finds the gold. If you dig my feet down a little, the dirt's cooler.

I do as I'm told. She's right. Definitely cooler.

And, yeah. In Hosea's position, I'd be more worried about food than shoes for my daughter. Guess he's too proud to ask for a little help.

He is. He does do work for people instead of digging sometimes, but he won't ask anyone to help us.

Where's your father now? In the mine?

No. The lawmen took him away for shooting the other two lawmen, but he didn't do it. Papa was in the mine looking for gold when the lawmen came to the house. The two men who wanted to hurt me shot them dead. I saw it. She breaks down, sobbing… though her tears are only sound in my mind.

I do my best to comfort her. Since we're presently sharing a brain—sort of—I've got a front row seat to her grief, pain, and fear. She hadn't fully processed watching two men shot in front of her before other men came to arrest her father for the crime… then a day later, the two killers came back for her. Not knowing what to do after the law took her father away, Dorothea had been staying alone at the house.

Charles and Micah needed to kill her in a way they could blame on Hosea. It's clear they hadn't had any sort of plan for how to do it before they abducted her. Lucky for me— luckier for her, now—they spent so long arguing. I'm too aware of what actually happened and trying not to think about it while inside her mind.

Dorothea's sobbing ebbs. She sniffles. *What happened?*

It's a long story.

You just don't want to tell me.

Yeah. It's bad.

Please? I promise I won't have nightmares.

I force myself to resume walking. Standing still is not healthy for us. Not until I know Dorothea's going to be safe. Those two might wake up at any minute and chase me. We have to get somewhere public before they wake up and come after her… me… us. Argh. This is too darn weird.

Okay, I'll tell you, but you have to promise to keep it a secret. No one is going to believe you if you try to explain this, and they might think you've gone mad.

Or made it up like a story since I'm only a child. A sad laugh echoes in my head. *I promise.*

My name is Allison Lopez. A long time in the future, a man asked me to help him because a ghost was bothering him. The ghost is your

Papa.

No...

I'm from so many years away you'd both have died of old age by then, even if no one hurt you.

Oh.

Your ghost is there, too. She, I mean you, told me an angel said you aren't supposed to die when you did... and it seems I'm helping things go back to the way they should have been. A demon attacked you, and they're not allowed to do that because you didn't summon it or let it into your mind willingly. So, when I did some magic using your ragdoll—I hold it up. Wow, it looks fairly new—I ended up inside your head... somehow. This is the first time anything like this has happened to me. I can't explain what, exactly, is going on at the moment. Kinda winging it.

Pastor Pearce says demons are everywhere, always waiting for men to become weak of mind.

He's right.

Am I weak of mind?

No, kiddo. Not at all. Your ghost knew I would help you.

If I'm not weak of mind, why are you talking in my head and why can't I move?

I'm sorry for scaring you. Jumping into your

head is the *last* thing I expected would happen. What year is it now?

1849. Papa brought Mama and me here looking for gold two years ago. Everyone is looking for gold now.

Where is your mother? Sorry if it's a bad question.

She sighs. *Mama went back to Boston a year ago. She hated it here in the desert. Used to spend all day in town working at the saloon so we could at least have money for food. Papa kept digging a hole in the ground, as she said, never findin' nothin' worth anythin'. She met a man at the saloon who doesn't want kids, but he's got money. She went with him. Didn't even say goodbye. Just left a letter with Mr. McKeney.*

Who?

He owns the saloon. Mr. McKeney is nice to me. Sometimes, he lets me have food, but Papa doesn't like it when I walk all the way to town on my own and ask for help. He's afraid some-one might hurt me.

Wow. I'm so sorry your mother did that to you.

It's okay. Mama didn't like me much, but Papa loves me enough for two parents.

Damn. There I go, crying again. How the heck am I going to stop them from—.

Stop who, from what?

People from doing something bad they shouldn't do.

Oh. I know what you mean. They're going to hang Papa for shootin' those lawmen, aren't they? Dorothea's grief is so powerful it's a stab to the heart.

Not if I can help it, kiddo.

I gaze up at the clearest blue sky I've ever seen. Not an airplane, helicopter, billboard, or wire in sight.

You say strange words, Allison Lopez.

I chuckle. Call me Allie.

Are you old?

Old is a state of mind.

So, you are old.

Not old. I stick my tongue out. I'm thirty-five.

I shouldn't just call you by your first name, Miss Allie. It isn't proper.

The last thing I want to do is make this girl any more uncomfortable than life already is. Call me whatever you want, but I give you permission to call me Allie. Besides, you're only thinking it. No one else can hear you.

Seems like she's smiling.

We're almost there, she says. *Who are you looking for in town?*

No one specific. If people see you alive and

unhurt while your father's in jail, the bad guys won't have any reason to hurt you because they can't lie and say your father did it.

Is that what happened in the future?

Yeah.

She starts crying again.

Hey, kiddo. Shh. Listen to me.

A mental sniffle cuts off the sobs.

Admittedly, I'm making a lot of guesses here. But follow me, okay?

I can't follow you. You're inside my head.

Heh. No, I mean follow my thinking.

All right.

I found your ragdoll in the future. Your ghost said it will help. So, I did magic using it to get a feel for what needed to be done, and I ended up here. This isn't a vision. I'm somehow actually here, in a way. My best guess is I've projected my consciousness back in time. We got away from the bad men, so they aren't going to hurt you anymore. Your ghost in the future told me she met an angel who said it wasn't time for you to die. I think—hope—we've gotten past that. You are not going to die today.

Sensing Dorothea's fear and desire for comfort, I hug the ragdoll. It seems to make her feel better.

We talk for a few minutes while walking,

mostly about my magic and if I really 'threw fire' out of my hand. Or her hand as it technically is. I explain the Creator made all sorts of wonderful things, including Gaia and people who can do magic.

It's strange. I can feel how sad you are from seeing my bones. You are a nice lady. No one in Augustown cares about people they've never met before, except Pastor Pearce.

He sounds like a nice guy.

He's a Pastor. He's gotta be nice to every one. That's his job.

I peer back over my shoulder every few minutes to check for bad guys. Seems they're still out cold, haven't bothered to chase me, or think we did something stupid and went to the house or the mine. Eventually, I spot a collection of buildings in the distance. Soon after that, we reach a crude hand-painted wood sign with the words: Augustown – pop 214.

Someone's painted over the population number multiple times, increasing it.

A few minutes after passing the sign, I arrive at a one-street town. It's so damn small it looks like the set of a movie Quentin Tarantino —or one of those directors who goes to extreme lengths would build; meaning, fully functional buildings, as opposed to merely fronts. I count twenty-two structures along a street and a half.

(There's a spur of a road jutting out to the left of the main drag a little past center.) The dirt road is well-rutted from stagecoach and wagon wheels, dry, and dusty.

How do 214 people live in such a small place?

Most of the people live out on their farms or ranches. Takes almost an hour to reach some of them on a horse. This is the downtown.

Ahh.

A few 'usual suspects' catch my eye: general store, barber shop, undertaker, sheriff's office, saloon, various shops, boutiques, and a handful of private residences, one of which is quite grand—for this place. It's the only three-story building, perched on the corner of the little spur street. Definitely the home of someone rich.

Speaking of the 'private residences,' fancy curtains in one grey building give off the unmistakable sense of a brothel. Dorothea—to my horror—blushes mentally at the word. Not sure she understands exactly what goes on in there, but she knows enough to be embarrassed.

People make God angry in there, whispers Dorothea.

Her tone is factual, not judgmental.

I suppose it's one way to look at it. People do what they have to do, and I suppose God leads them down whatever path he feels is best for them.

That's what Pastor Pearce says. We should pity them without scorn. If we hate sinners, we're as bad as they are. They need help and comfort, not pointing fingers.

I smile and leave it at that.

People going by either ignore me—us—or give sympathetic looks. Small town like this? Yeah, everyone knows who Dorothea is and about her father being in jail. Of course, no one is making an effort to actually help her and, like, offer to take her in, give her a place to live, or even a meal.

They might take me in if I asked. But Papa isn't dead yet. I can't go to Boston. Mama won't let me stay with her if she's still with her new man.

Grr.

I head over to the sheriff's office. Following a hunch, I walk into the narrow space between it and a shop selling horse supplies. Six basement windows, with bars, line the side of the building. One by one, I crouch to peer in. First cell's got a drunk in it. Second, a younger guy who's pacing around and grumbling. Looks drunk to me. Hosea's in the third cell, seated on the cot, head in his hands.

"Hosea?" I whisper.

He lifts his head to look at me, his expression shocked. "What did you call me, young lady?"

Ack. Oops. "Sorry. Don't be angry at your daughter for using your name. I'm—"

Hosea leaps to his feet, runs to the window, and grabs my hand. "Look, Lady Bug, you get yourself over to Isaiah Pearce, see if he'll take ya in. Don't go back ta our house alone."

The man's barely holding back tears. He knows he's not getting out of the cell alive—at least, he'll only be alive long enough to go from the cell to the gallows.

I reach through and pat his thick, square hand. "I need you to listen and keep an open mind. I'm here to help you and Dorothea. I know you didn't shoot the marshal and a deputy."

Hosea squeezes my fingers, lip quivering. "Lady Bug, you gotta stop talkin' like that. All right? Don't let your mind break. Just go to Isaiah. He'll look after ya proper like."

"Listen to me. The same two men who really killed the marshal just tried to hurt Dorothea. I've somehow sent myself into the past to help…"

Watching Hosea's expression shift into disbelief and anguish steals the words from my mouth. Dammit. He thinks his daughter's going insane.

"Honey, Lady Bug, I know it's rough." He reaches up and brushes a hand over my head. "You're just havin' an episode. It'll go away. Don't talk any of that nonsense around Isaiah, or anyone else, all right? You're gonna be fine."

This feels awkward as heck, but... "Papa, I saw the men shoot the marshal. You were in the mine when they did it. They tried to kill me, too, but I got away."

For an instant, I half expect Hosea to tear the window bars out bare handed. He tries, but can't. Head bowed, he emits a moan of rage and frustration. "Claiborne's... oh, never mind. What's done is done. Just go to Isaiah and don't give them any reason to hurt you."

"But, Papa..."

He lifts his head, staring into my eyes. Tears slide down his weathered cheeks, vanishing into unshaven stubble. "Don't tell anyone what you saw. If you do, they're gonna kill you, too. Don't matter if I end up swingin', long as you're okay."

Papa! wails Dorothea inside my head.

Since releasing control of her body isn't an option, I try to hug Hosea as best I can through the bars —because it's what she's trying to do.

No, Papa! I gotta tell them the truth. I can't lose you, too.

I repeat her words exactly. Doesn't matter how good an actress I am. This is real. I'm crying as much as Dorothea and Hosea are.

"It's Claiborne. He's got them all in his pocket. I know it's hard, Lady Bug, but all it's gonna do is get you dead, too. You promise me, stay quiet. Go to Isaiah and live the best life you can."

"Claiborne? As in Claiborne Loughton?"

Hosea stares at me while Dorothea continues sobbing in my head. "You gotta stop talkin' funny or people will think there's somethin' wrong in your mind."

Footsteps approach the cell inside the building.

"Go," rasps Hosea. "Don't be seen here. If they tried to hurt you once, they'll try again. Get to Isaiah's and hide until this is all over. It don't matter none what happens to me. You gotta stay safe."

It matters, Papa! I love you. Can't lose you like we lost Mama.

I barely manage to choke out her words. Hosea starts to break down, but shoves us away hard enough to fling me onto my back.

A male voice yells, "Who you talkin' to?"

Hosea rests his head against the bars, blocking the window. "Prayin' for the good Lord to give you boys a lick of sense so ya's understand I didn't shoot no one. I swear, Travers, ya ain't got the common sense God gave a scorpion."

Dorothea's an absolute bawling mess. Admittedly, I'm not in much better shape, but I'm together enough to scramble to my feet and take off before any lawmen can come out to see me. I run past the back of the building, crossing a dirt lot with a few horses in it, before veering left and heading toward the little spur road branching away from the main drag. A stagecoach nearly runs me over when I dart out into the street from between two buildings. The driver shakes his fist at me, shouting something incomprehensible but probably full of swear words. As soon as the coach passes, I scramble the rest of the way across the road, heading for the gap between a barber shop and a tailor. Once out of sight, I curl up behind a rain barrel. Dorothea's dread, fear, and pain are so strong I can't help myself but to shake and cry right along with her.

I think I've figured out why this weird 'vision' didn't end the moment Dorothea got away from the men trying to kill her.

I'm not finished here yet.

Chapter Thirteen
Augustown

Dorothea eventually cries herself out once the spike of emotion fades.

I do my best to be as reassuring as possible without making promises out of my reach. This is all new territory for me, so my understanding of what could potentially happen here is pretty much nil. I'd like to believe this isn't me falling asleep in the Spirit Chair and having a vivid-as-hell dream. How likely is it a witch could project their consciousness back in time and change the past? I've never heard of it before.

Okay, it's kinda stupid to say. Really, if someone changed the past, we'd never know because the 'new' past would be the only past anyone would remember in the future. Time stuff is always brain smashing. I can't waste hours trying to make sense of something scientists much smarter than me still haven't figured out when I'm presently trying to help an innocent child stay alive. Even if it is all in my head, I'd feel bad if things went wrong.

Dorothea's ghost told me she saw an angel, and the angel told her she shouldn't have died when she did. Something like that is a bit esoteric for an eleven-year-old to make up, so I'm going to take it as truth. Heck, I've met at least one angel already—Gorgeous George—so we're well past the 'burden of proof' point. Charles Clapp was possessed by a demon. Oh, damn... Nick Birch, the historian, told me about letters written by a guy named Charles Clapp— with two p's. It has to be the same man. No wonder he kept quiet so long. It could've been more than simple fear about what the Loughton family would do to him. Charles *couldn't* confess until he'd rid himself of the demon.

Really? An angel told you I wasn't supposed to die?

Didn't I tell you already?

Umm, yes, but I was upset and not really listening.

I spend a while telling her about Gorgeous George and my adventure on the cruise ship with the Jaguar God. If an angel says it's not her time, it's not her time. Normally, I don't have the power to play around and alter history, but perhaps being dragged back here isn't something my witchcraft did as much as her guardian angel giving me a push. Why it took 171 years for him or her to step in... who knows? As far as Dorothea is aware, she didn't have to wait so long for help. Wow, that's kinda brain-numbing to think about. How many people die, then someone hundreds of years later does something like this and fixes it so the person never realizes what happened?

Whoa. Okay. I'll take 'things not to think about to avoid going insane' for $400.

My—technically   Dorothea's—stomach growls.

When was the last time you ate?

Yesterday. Papa was fixin' to do some work around Mr. Ralston's farm today so he'd get some pay, but he's in jail.

C'mon. Let's get you some food. Or me some food. Or whatever.

She manages a weak laugh.

I crawl out of our hiding spot behind the rain barrel and walk to the end of the gap between buildings. People wander by, some on the street, some going from porch to porch in front of the shops to stay out of the sun. All the buildings down the main drag have large, covered porches the full width of the structures. They kind of form a 'sidewalk' of sorts, except for the gaps between stores... but they all have steps on the sides.

Maybe we can kill two birds with one stone here. Part of my plan to protect Dorothea is to make sure people see her alive while her father's in jail. Other than simple cruelty, I can think of two reasons Claiborne hired those men to kill her. One: having a daughter who would become an orphan if he's hung might lend him sympathy to a jury. Two: if he can make it look like Hosea murdered her, it will further turn the town against him. Oh, and three: he might not want Dorothea to grow up and try to come after him for revenge.

Of course, if what Nick said about Claiborne owning the justice in this place is true, it probably doesn't matter... which brings me back to simple cruelty. Could be the demon inside Charles Clapp merely wanted an innocent soul.

They say pride is a sin. Maybe it is. Either way, I kinda have it to a point. The idea of begging bothers me, but I've also never been a starving child. Growing up, I had plenty of food. Never worried about where my next meal came from. Reminding myself I am not me at the moment, but essentially playing the role of

Dorothea Povey, I approach random people and plead with them, asking for food, pointing out my father's in jail, and making sure they know I'm alive. If anyone tries to ignore me or walk away, I grab their arm, mostly out of a desire to make sure they remember seeing me.

I avoid anyone who looks overtly hostile, drunk, dirt poor, or those Dorothea has an instinctual fear of. It doesn't take much more than an hour to explore all of Augustown, at least the business district. It would take several days—and a horse—to explore every ranch or farm in the surrounding area considered to be part of this town. I've never heard of this place before, even in history class. It's gotta be a Gold Rush settlement built fast, and fated to disappear just as fast. The dust swallowed lots of small Old West towns. Mine runs out, everyone leaves.

They named it after Augustus Dees, says Dorothea in my head. *He found a lot of gold around here, so they named the town after him. That's what Papa said. He's sure there's gold in our mine, but he hasn't found it yet. What happens in the future?*

Umm... Claiborne Loughton found gold in the mine only a few days after your father, umm...

Died. I know. She gives a sad mental sigh.

Only days after? Papa almost found it?

Seems like it. I don't know if Claiborne dug in a different direction or what. However, you and your father might end up being rich if I can figure out how to clear him.

I don't care about money. I need my Papa.

Yes, you do.

But they're going to hang him.

Don't give up yet. Aww, heck. If it comes down to it, I can always go extreme.

What does that mean?

It means, if I can't figure out a way to clear your father's name, I start throwing fireballs. It's really not a great option because everyone here is going to blame you for being a witch. You and your father would end up being hunted and would probably have to flee all the way to Mexico.

I'd prefer to live in Mexico with Papa than stay here and let him die, but I don't want you to kill anyone.

Good, because I don't want to kill anyone, either. Demons, monsters, bad ghosts... those I will blow up, no problem. Honestly, if I *had* to kill someone to protect my life or the life of an innocent, I could do it. But conducting a frontal assault on a whole town to save a wrongfully accused man from death is... oh, I'm being stupid.

How?

I won't let things reach the point where they're about to hang him. If we can't convince the cops or the judge he's innocent, we sneak in at night before they're going to hang him. I'll put the sheriff to sleep and we sneak away real quiet like. Wow, here for a short time, and already I'm talking like the locals.

Yes, you are. And I like this plan more!

Okay, still need food.

I turn around at the end of the street and backtrack toward the saloon. A few people earlier gave me some pennies. Not sure how much food costs in 1849. Thirteen cents probably isn't going to go too far.

Ugh, it's hot, too. Even in this thin, ratty dress, I'm roasting. Looking at other people, especially the women in their high-collared, floor-length dresses, makes me feel even hotter. One advantage to being a poor kid no one notices is Dorothea gets to wear a sackcloth that won't give her heat stroke. No one cares if the poor girl shows her knees. To avoid the sunbaked road burning my—her—soles, I hop up on the porch of a gun store, the closest building, and follow the crazy sort of elevated sidewalk. Spaces between porches vary from short enough to jump across to about the width of a one-lane road.

For the most part, the adults in the area don't pay much attention to me. Dorothea looks a little young for her age. Not sure at what point kids stopped being 'children' and took on actual responsibilities back in this time, but we haven't gotten any dirty looks for roaming around idle yet.

Papa said I could start working after my birthday when I'm twelve. Cleaning houses, maybe.

Ugh. Poor kid. Yeah, I know. Different time, different mores. To me, twelve-year-olds are still children who shouldn't have any worries more than schoolwork and having fun... not holding down jobs so they don't starve.

Right as I leap from the general store's porch to the saloon's porch, I catch sight of a well-dressed man standing out in the street. Dorothea has a reflexive fear reaction to him, and to be honest, so do I. Maybe I've already spent too much time in the body of a child, but I grab the post at the corner of the porch, hiding behind it so the man doesn't see me. The scent of dusty old paint fills my nose as I peer around the square column. A small barrel with several coils of rope on top of it stands next to me, so I crouch lower, using it for cover.

The guy's in the intersection where Augustown's two streets connect, close to the steps leading up to the porch of the fancy three-story house. He's handsome in a sinister sort of way and looks to be a year or two shy of thirty. Exudes superiority. Black suit with a violet derby, black hair, thin moustache, and he carries one of those ostentatious straight black canes with the silver ball at the top. If I wasn't actually *in* the Old West, I'd be laughing at the guy dressed like an obvious villain.

The worst part, though, is the feeling he gives off: demonic.

His energy is different from Charles Clapp, not as 'in my face,' so I'm not sure this guy is possessed. He's certainly not a demon in the flesh, either. The evil wafting off him isn't strong enough. Part of me wants to say he's a sorcerer, a dark witch, or something similar. This guy might even be the one who summoned the demon I destroyed earlier.

He's talking to a man in his late fifties, also well-dressed in a suit, vest, silver pocket watch, and a black derby. The older guy isn't throwing off an air of high-society wealth like purple-hat dude. His presence conveys authority, but doesn't fill me with the urge to hide. I still want to avoid him, though. Dorothea's afraid of him as much as the younger man. The impression I get from her thoughts makes him sound like a mean old school principal who'd paddle any child he thinks is even slightly misbehaving, whether they deserved it or not.

That's Claiborne.

I stare at the old guy.

Not him.

Purple hat guy is Claiborne Loughton? Wow, he looks so young. Who's the other guy?

I don't know who the old man is.

Claiborne's too far away for me to hear what they're talking about. His body language conveys a sense of being pleased. He laughs like an oil baron who's just kicked a dozen poor families out of their homes so he could build a new, expensive hotel. The older man doesn't share his amusement, though also doesn't appear to object. It's almost like he can't stand Claiborne's presence and wants to leave, but doesn't want to offend him or is too curious to see what happens next. However, despite the seeming deference, the older guy doesn't look at all intimidated. More like a father waiting for his spoiled son to stop prattling nonsense.

"Oh, Ardelia, look," whispers a woman behind me.

I peer back at a pair of women stepping onto the saloon porch behind me. They're both about my age—my *actual* age, mid-thirties—wearing suffocating high-collared dresses, one lavender, one white.

"Hmm?" asks the woman in white, presumably Ardelia.

"The Hangman's just been bought again." Lavender dress woman twirls her parasol while clucking disapprovingly. "Only justice around here is money."

I duck behind the barrel so Claiborne can't see me from the street at all and face the women. "Hangman?"

They jump, startled at Dorothea's little voice.

"Aww, you poor dear," says Ardelia.

"Judge Salem Boothe," says White Dress. "Loves the noose, he does. It's why they call him the Hangman."

"Gretchen!" rasps Ardelia. "Be sensitive. This is Hosea's daughter."

"Oh. I am sorry." Gretchen curtsies to me. "Terrible shame, that."

Red-faced, she scurries off along the porch. Ardelia gives me a helpless look, then follows her. Hmm. Claiborne talking to the judge who's going to preside over Hosea's trial. No, nothing at all suspicious there. Totally normal.

I stretch up from my crouch, peering over the railing at the two men. Claiborne shakes hands with Judge Boothe, a.k.a. the Hangman. Looks like two men are arranging a deal, all right. The Hangman walks off to the right.

Claiborne grasps his lapels, gazing around at Augustown with a giant smile as if he owns the place. I duck before he can look toward the saloon.

Dorothea breaks down in tears again. *They're gonna kill Papa!*

No, they're not. Shh. They want to, but I'm not going to let them.

How are you going to stop them? You're a voice in my head and I'm too little to fight grown men.

I put a hand on my growling stomach. I'm a voice in your head *with magic*. Trust me.

Chapter Fourteen
Claiborne Loughton

Claiborne smugly trots back up the stairs into his giant house.

I stand out from behind the barrel, take a breath, and walk into the saloon. It's almost shocking to see they *don't* have one of those stereotypical swingy doors you see in every Old West Movie. Just a normal door, but it's propped open. A light crowd, maybe twenty people or so, hangs around playing cards at tables, drinking, smoking, and conversing. Surprisingly, no one tries to chase me off or even looks at me—Dorothea—with a 'what are you doing in here?' glare.

A weak fragrance of cooking food drowns

under the stink of cigar smoke, booze, and damp wood.

Oh, right. No one is giving Dorothea crazy looks because I'm in the Old West. Pretty sure they let anyone tall enough to see over the bar have beer. Dorothea can't *quite* see over the top of the bar yet. She is a little short for her age. But it doesn't matter. We're not here to drink.

Alcohol is bad. Papa says it makes people do bad things and stop thinking.

No point getting into a debate about vice and virtue with a child from another era, so I simply respond with 'yeah, he's right.' Technically, alcohol *does* make some people do dumb things.

That's Mr. McKeney. Dorothea mentally 'points' at a ginger-haired man behind the bar who's pushing forty. *Papa calls him Josep, but please don't. Call him Mr. McKeney. I know you're a grown-up, but I'm not. Mama used to work for him, and he's always been nice to me.*

Okay.

The least I can do is not mess up her world any more. Even if it's a bit embarrassing to behave like a little kid, it's better for her if I 'play the role' so to speak. Pretty sure Charles and Micah won't tell anyone they saw Dorothea 'throw a fireball,' because in order to admit such a thing, they'd need to admit they tried to kill her. Also, they'd most likely be considered insane or drunk for accusing a child of throwing fireballs.

I walk up to the bar, clasp my hands in front of myself, and stare pleadingly up at Josep McKeney until he notices me standing there. The man's already ruddy complexion reddens a touch more.

"Oy, hon. You all right?"

"No. Papa didn't do what they say he did."

"Well, I reckon not, but... truth don't matter as much as what they can prove. Sad all around."

I show him the handful of pennies. "Is this enough for something to eat? Haven't had any food since yesterday."

"Aww, girl, ya know better. G'won put them away." Josep walks out from behind the bar, rests a hand on my shoulder, and guides me to a small table all the way in the back corner. "Have a seat, child. I'll fetch ya somethin'"

"Thank you, Mr. McKeney. You're a kind man."

He gives me a sad smile, then walks off. Dorothea thinks about a night he came to the house to talk to Papa, offering help and saying how he thought it a shame her mother ran off to Boston with a man she'd only known a month.

I sit there watching the room, the ragdoll on

the table in front of me. Clouds of cigar and pipe smoke rise in trails to the ceiling, gathering in a haze beneath a yellowed tin-covered ceiling. This town can't be very old, yet the white paint is already stained. No one other than the owner of the place has paid me any mind. Dorothea's dress doesn't have any pockets, so I sit there shifting the pennies from one hand to another, listening to people talk about cattle, farm stuff, the search for gold, stories of someone hitting it big in San Francisco. One guy thinks he's wasting his time out here. His friend believes since everyone's looking for gold closer to the coast, they have the advantage here. Fewer people means more chances to find the gold. Another man tells a woman how he's brought a thousand copies of a recent newspaper from New York City, planning to sell them for a dollar apiece to miners. He figures they're so thirsty for news of civilization he's going to make a fortune. She thinks he's got a good idea, then tells him about some old guy who died owing over forty thousand dollars, but due to the Gold Rush, his property sold for ten times that. His daughter is now quite wealthy.

Wow. I thought real estate in San Francisco was crazy in the modern age. Sounds like it's always been pricey.

Josep walks over, sets a plate in front of me,

and pats me on the head. "There ya are, Doro-thea. Can't imagine what yer goin' through. You let me know if I can help, okay?"

"Thank you, Mr. McKeney."

"I got a little room you can have if, uhh, things don't work out so well for your pa. Ya get a little older and you can help me run the place. Don't you go over by Maude's. Ain't no life for anyone."

I'm going to assume Maude is the local madam. Even if she has the best intentions in regard to taking Dorothea in, a young girl growing up in a place like that is starting off on a road with one unpleasant destination.

What's a madam?

Grown up stuff I'm not going to explain to you.

Oh. Okay.

"Thank you. Papa wanted me to see Pastor Pearce and ask him to look after me."

Josep chuckles. "Aye. Hosea would, would-n't he? Ya might be better off there. This lot sometimes gets a bit rowdy." He gestures at a bullet hole in the ceiling. "Probably be safer for you with Isaiah, but you're welcome here if ya need. Ain't gonna let you end up havin' nowhere ta be." He smiles before leaving me to the food and going back to the bar.

The meal's plain baked ham with a potato,

but it smells wonderful. Dorothea's so damn hungry, I end up drooling. Since I still can't seem to give her control of the body we're presently sharing, I eat for her. So weird. At least I share her hunger, so it's not like I'm overstuffing myself.

While eating, I tell Dorothea about myself in somewhat greater detail, explaining how I'm a nature witch who uses magic to fight bad things. She'd believed up to this point witches are evil, so I take the time to clarify there *are* bad witches, but we aren't *all* bad or even ill-tempered. Witchcraft is like a spoken language: many forms.

She gets sad again at the mention of me talking to her ghost.

If I spoke to you in the future, does that mean those men killed me? You thought about finding my bones.

Sigh. Yes. I spoke to your ghost. But it's a mistake. The angel said you shouldn't have died. Because a demon did it, it doesn't count or something. I dunno exactly what's going on, but I... think you might be okay now.

How are you going to help Papa?

My plan right now is to try to prove your father's innocence before they, umm...

Dorothea's heart sinks. *They call the judge The Hangman... I know what they're going to do.*

Heavy booted footsteps tromp along the porch outside. I glance up as Claiborne Loughton enters the saloon. He removes his violet derby, tucking it under his arm while flashing a brief smile at everyone on his way to the bar. Leaning on his cane—it's purely for show, not mobility—he strikes up a conversation with Josep.

I don't like him.

Understandable. I wouldn't like someone who's been trying to steal my home and tried to kill me, either.

He thinks he can do whatever he wants because he has a lot of money.

Yeah, not much has changed in 170 years. People with lots of money are still like that.

Papa said Mr. Loughton made Augustus himself leave town, and took all his money. He hired all the men who built everything here. Before Mr. Loughton arrived, we only had this saloon, one general store, the jail, and the city hall. Augustus settled the town before Papa and I got here. I don't know how long ago. Mr. Loughton came to town two weeks after Mama left.

Wow, this whole downtown happened in under a year? This place sprang up fast.

Mr. Loughton isn't a nice man. I saw him

hitting a lady once.

An image drifts to the front of Dorothea's memory: Claiborne standing on the porch of his house beside a young woman. He's holding a fistful of her hair, shaking her while shouting angrily. After a few seconds, he slaps her across the face hard enough to knock her to her knees before storming inside, leaving her there. To my adult sensibilities, it looks like he violently dumped his girlfriend. Honestly, she's better off.

He can't have a girlfriend. He's married, but his wife isn't here.

Oh. He violently dumped a mistress... or maybe fired a housekeeper.

I hurriedly finish off the rest of the food. Dorothea doesn't like being in the same room with this guy, and honestly, neither do I.

Claiborne pulls away from the bar and starts walking to a table... but stops after three steps, staring at me. He appears calm, but something about his expression conveys a casual 'oh, what are you doing alive? You're supposed to be dead' sort of vibe.

The instant we lock eyes, I feel like the victim in a horror movie seeing the killer right before the chase scene starts.

Oh, crap.

Chapter Fifteen
The Pastor's Wife

Being in a child's body makes me handle situations a bit differently from how I would normally.

If Allison Lopez happened to be here in person, I'd have no trouble getting in this guy's face and staring him down. However, eleven-year-old Dorothea Povey's body is going to end up cashing any checks my attitude writes. I can't allow that to happen. She's saturated with dread from this guy. Can't blame her. This dude is creepy as hell. I swear if the Devil himself came to Augustown, this is him. Only, the 'bad vibes' he's throwing off supernaturally are way too wimpy to be coming from the Prince of

Darkness.

He's more like the Prince of Poor Interior Lighting.

Still, I do *not* like him staring at me. He's giving me this glare like he thinks he might just pull out a gun and finish me off right here... and somehow get away with it.

Much like the child I appear to be, I panic, grab the ragdoll in one hand, the remaining half of my baked potato in the other, and haul ass out the back door without looking to see what, if anything, Claiborne does. A few chickens scurry away from me as I sprint across the lot behind the saloon, jump a short fence, and keep running. Unfortunately, Augustown is surrounded by open scrubland offering no obvious places to hide... so I stick close to town.

Once we reach the last building on the street, I duck behind the corner, pressing my back to it and trying to catch my breath. After a minute of listening for footsteps, and hearing no one chasing me, I take a defiant bite of my half-potato. Fear's given way to anger. Dorothea, though, is still terrified. I'm the one who's angry.

Hate having to run away.

But... I'm not about to whip a fireball out in the middle of a crowded saloon, especially when this child is going to suffer the consequences. If I did so, it wouldn't surprise me if she ended up on the gallows next to her father.

Dorothea bursts into tears—again, mentally. Outwardly, I—we—appear calm, if a bit winded.

No… no… I meant if they saw you—me—using magic to hurt Claiborne. Not going to do that. Please calm down.

She takes a moment to collect herself.

We need a safe place to think.

Papa wanted me to go to Pastor Pearce.

Okay, sounds like a reasonable idea. Do you trust the man?

Yes.

Great. Where is he?

He lives about a half-mile away. We have to go all the way back across downtown and follow the wagon road.

All right. Think about where to go, and I'll follow your directions.

I poke my head out past the corner of the building, a dress shop, to check for stage-coaches, wagons, or horses. Coast is clear, so I hurry across the street, going around to the back of the other line of buildings. Since we have to go across the town again, I want to stay as far away from Claiborne as possible. Following Dorothea's thoughts, I jog past the row of structures until we leave downtown behind, then slow to a purposeful walk.

The saying 'find a needle in a haystack' has a runner up: find a dirt road in the desert. Every so often, I encounter a short stretch where it kinda looks like horses or wagons go by on a somewhat regular basis, but it's pretty much impossible for my modern eyes to perceive any sort of continuous road. The only good thing is we're traversing mostly flat ground. At least the sun's starting to go down, cooling it off a bit. My feet aren't burning on contact with the dirt anymore.

So weird to think about a kid this age wandering off on her own. Even weirder to wrap my brain around the idea she doesn't even own a pair of shoes... and probably only has one or two dresses.

I've got more than that. Some nice ones Mama bought for me before we came out here. But I don't take them out of the trunk on account they'll get dirty. I do own a pair of shoes, but they're too small for me. The dresses are probably too small for me now, too. To distract herself from feeling sad about her mother, she switches gears. *Why is it strange for me to be walking alone?*

The world's a different place in my time. Everyone is protective of children. We're afraid bad people might try to hurt them, so people get worried if kids are left alone.

Oh. That's nice. I don't want to be hurt by bad people. She pauses a moment. *How did they kill me?*

Why do you want to know? It doesn't matter because it didn't happen.

You said they blamed Papa for doing it.

Yeah. Doesn't mean much. You saw the judge talking to Claiborne. It's not going to be a fair trial.

How can we get Papa back if it won't be fair?

We have to stop it from going to trial. Get the cops to realize they have the wrong man… which might be difficult if they're on the take, too.

Cops?

Umm, lawmen. We call them cops in the future.

Oh. Is it okay if I'm scared?

Yes. It's fine to be scared.

It's still strange how I can't move, but that doesn't scare me anymore.

Sorry. Barging into your body and taking over wasn't my plan.

Thank you for saving me from those men. I'd never been so scared before.

You're welcome. I push the memory aside. Don't want to even think about how terrifying it must have been for her... especially without me somehow ending up inside her head. I stop myself from imagining being tossed into the mine shaft so Dorothea doesn't 'overhear' and get a theoretical memory she's thankfully never going to experience.

I hope.

Again, I'm assuming this is real and not merely me having a dream to deal with the emotion of finding her bones. A chance exists I'm editing reality in my own mind to convince myself she didn't really die as a way of processing my sadness. Too many people here are acting too realistically for *everything* to be a dream. I haven't exactly watched a ton of western movies, so if this all came from my dream imagination, it would have probably been way off. Like cowboys wearing Nikes.

What are Nikes?

It's a kind of shoe.

Oh. Pastor Pearce lives in that house over there, by the way.

I look up. Two buildings stand close together a short distance ahead of me at the top of a shallow hill. One's clearly a simple chapel type structure, little more than a giant box with a steeple. The other's a nice two-story house. Looks like a fairly decent place to live except for being surrounded by desert. At least they have a well on the property. I'm guessing the people who live in Augustown built their houses so spread out because they settled wherever well digging proved successful.

Papa and I get our water from a creek. Comes down from the hills behind the house.

As I approach the residence, a strange foreboding sense of darkness comes over me. It's as if I'm looking at the house from *Amityville.* Okay, maybe not quite as scary, but similar.

I stop about fifty feet from the residence, raise my hands out in front of me, and cast a sensing spell, searching for paranormal energies. Two things strike me as odd. The church feels no different from any other house, and the pastor's home is giving off negative energy with a noticeable demonic whiff.

What the heck? How on Earth is a demon living in a pastor's house?

I felt something strange in my head, Miss Allie. What did you do?

Magic. It lets me sense other magic and supernatural things.

Why do you think it's strange the church feels normal?

Because it's a church. It ought to give off a charge. Sanctified ground has power. This church is not standing on sanctified ground.

Fortunately, it doesn't feel like de-sanctified ground. Formerly holy ground turned corrupt is some serious nasty mojo. That, I'd sense. For whatever reason, Pastor Pearce hasn't sanctified the place. Explains how a demon could be here, but not *why*. Could be the 'pastor' is not really a pastor. Could also be he's lazy, but I don't think a true pastor would be so lazy as to not get around to sanctifying his church.

Shouldn't it be like step one right after they built it?

Yes, I would think so.

Pastor Pearce is a nice man. He brings us food sometimes, talks to Papa about God and such. He helped Papa understand why Mama left and not be so angry.

Dorothea's thoughts of the man are nothing but positive. Con artists are often genuinely nice to those who they can gain nothing from. Doesn't prove Pearce's motivations aren't noble, but something isn't right here. If he isn't a swindler pretending to be clergy, I have questions.

Do you feel something strange about the house, Dorothea?

Yes. But it didn't always scare me.

Has it been scary for long?

No. Last Sunday it wasn't. I've never been inside the house, though. Only the church.

Curious, I sneak up to the gap between the

two buildings and start peeking in windows, hunting for the source of the bad energy. Parlor, no one in it. Next window is a dining room, no one there. The third, and last, window on this side of the house looks in on a small bedroom. As with the other two rooms, the décor is austere, purely for function, not style. A woman in her young twenties reclines on the bed, still wearing a plain chartreuse dress with ruffled cuffs and collar. She looks exhausted, more than a little out of it, and kinda high.

A dark brown, short and fat medicine type bottle sits on a table beside the bed next to a spoon. I stand up on my toes for a better look. Can't make out the small writing, but the words 'laudanum tincture' across the top of the label are big enough to read. Sounds kinda familiar. It's gotta be some kind of narcotic. Poor woman looks like someone who just shot up heroin.

What's heroin?

Nothing you need to worry about, hon.

Is it medicine?

Sigh. No. Well, it's similar to medicine but it's bad. It's a drug people take to escape reality. Even if you live into your nineties, you'll be gone before it's widespread. You really don't need to worry about it because it won't exist in your world. I think it came out in the Sixties, as in 1960.

Wow. More than a hundred years away.

Yes. Do you recognize her?

That's Mrs. Pearce. I think her first name is Queenie. She's always sad.

How come?

I've heard people talking, but it's bad to gossip.

It's only gossiping when you talk about someone to make fun of them or spread rumors. Knowing why she's on laudanum might help me get your father out of jail.

All right. She's sad because she doesn't like being out here in the desert away from her family. Papa thinks she's going to leave the pastor the way Mama left us. Mrs. Pearce misses her family, but Mama just hated the desert and liked being with a rich man.

I can't help but think of Liz Turner, the poor woman who ended up possessed by a dark entity, which drove her to murder a store clerk during a robbery. Once the demon realized Liz would be stuck in prison for decades, it killed her. Forced her to bite off her tongue and bleed to death. Eek.

I think between the lack of sanctified ground here and Queenie's drug habit, a demon found its way into her mind.

Ugh. Augustown has a serious problem... and its name is Claiborne Loughton.

He *has* to be the source of the demons. One, he's legit giving off paranormal 'creep vibes.' Two, one of the men who tried to hurt Dorothea had a demon possessing him, and he works for Claiborne. Judge Salem Boothe—The Hangman —might be possessed too, even if I didn't sense anything on him at the time. He'd been standing right next to Claiborne, who gave off so much darkness he'd been obscuring the signal, so to speak. Assuming, of course, Judge Boothe *has* a signal. Some bad men are servants of money and don't need supernatural darkness in their heads to do evil.

No wonder the angel gave Dorothea a 'get out of death free' card... this place is crawling with demons.

And now... Queenie.

I stare at her listless expression, trying to get a psychic read on how far gone to demonic possession she might be. Long, dark chestnut brown hair drapes half over her face. Her eyes are half-lidded, neither awake nor asleep. I knew some people in Las Vegas growing up who spent most of their lives high, and this woman is definitely catching the planetary express into the cosmos.

"Dorothea?" calls a man right behind me.

The child emits a shriek of surprise, startling me more than the dude sneaking up on me. I spin, putting my back to the wall, both hands clamped over my heart. Already on edge from the demonic energy here, having the crap scared out of me freaks me out too much to do anything more than stare up at the guy for a moment.

He's got a disarming presence, which lets me gather control of my wits pretty fast. As Dorothea confirms this is Pastor Pearce, I get a read on him. The man seems to be in his mid-twenties—young for a pastor. He's got kind of a longish face and small nose, chin on the pointy side, but kind eyes. Short blond hair and silver wire-rim glasses give him a bit of an intellectual look. Dorothea likes him quite a bit. It's a good sign when a child trusts someone at first sight. Kids can sense bad apples... usually.

Also, no demonic energy wafting off him.

"You scared me," I whisper.

"What are you doing sneaking around?" asks Pastor Pearce. "Queenie and I have been worried sick about you ever since we heard."

"Sorry... just checking to see if you were home."

"Knocking would have been fine. Hmm. Are you all right, Dorothea? You seem a little out of sorts."

Deep breath. I step away from the wall toward him. "We really need to talk."

Chapter Sixteen
Belief, Hope, and Peace

Pastor Isaiah Pearce regards me with a confused expression.

"Seriously," I say, starting to walk off to the left, away from the house. "This town has issues."

"Are you feeling unwell, child?" The pastor follows.

"No, I'm fine. But there are some things going on you really ought to know about."

"Why are you speaking in such a strange manner? You don't sound like yourself."

I wave for him to continue walking. "I'll explain. But not here."

He's hesitant, but curious and/or concerned

enough not to stop.

Once I'm sure Queenie—or more accurately, the entity attached to her—cannot hear us, I stop and face him. Okay, so, I'm in 1849. Good chance using the word 'witch' is not going to go over well. Hopefully, the powers that be won't mind a little innocent twisting of the truth. Besides, I'm ninety percent sure my magic cannot catapult me back in time, so Dorothea's guardian angel must've brought me here. If so, I'm technically deputized.

"Pastor Pearce, this is going to be a little difficult for you to hear, but I need you to keep an open mind, okay?"

"I'm starting to become quite concerned for your welfare, Dorothea. Your father... everything going on, yet you don't appear to be the least bit vexed."

"Heh. Trust me, she's vexed. She's *beyond* vexed."

"She?"

I nod. "Yes. You are not talking to Dorothea at the moment. I'm her guardian angel. To help her during a bad time, I've borrowed her body. Two men were about to kill Dorothea until I intervened."

He chuckles.

"What do you find funny about that?"

"Oh, child. I understand you are going

through a trying time. Making up stories about angels isn't going to help."

I blink. "Wait… you don't believe me?"

Oh, wait! No wonder the church isn't sanctified—the man isn't a true believer.

He sits on the ground next to me, and pats the dirt nearby.

I sit.

"Look, Dorothea. The world is a hard place sometimes. People all over, in every age, needed a way to deal with the things they feel are out of their control. Angels, demons, god, ancestor spirits… what's really going on is just people searching for a way to explain the unexplainable. It's comfort."

"Wow." I gawk, dumbfounded. "You're a pastor and you don't even believe in God?"

Dorothea gasps inside my head.

He shrugs. "I want to. But I feel religion is a necessary service to provide people hope and peace. I don't believe in it literally, but I believe in its message. People need support and comfort. My calling is to offer that. What does it matter if I find some of the folklore behind it a little fanciful? The message is still good."

Oh, no… is he going to Hell, Allie?

I don't think so. The Creator doesn't force anyone to do anything, and Pastor Pearce's heart is in the right place. This man *does* sound quite compassionate and empathetic. I'm guessing he was hurt by something, perhaps he's so caring the mere existence of evil itself horrifies him. I turn my psychic feelers on him. He's thinking about wanting religion to be true, but constantly seeing examples of cruelty and suffering which make him question God. Despite it, he's driven to keep helping people even though the things he's seen have horrified him. For all the kindness, reassurance, and hope he's given people, the man desperately needs a rock of his own to cling to. Perhaps a little nudge is in order.

"Can I ask you a question?"

Isaiah smiles. "Of course, child."

"What is your explanation for this?" I throw a small fireball into the dirt a few feet away from us.

He jumps, blinks, then stares at me.

I summon another one, this time letting the flaming ball hover over my hand for a moment before launching it harmlessly into the dirt.

"Pastor, I want you to know that what you are seeing is *not* coming from Dorothea. When I am gone, she won't be anything more than an ordinary child. I'm here because your town has a demon problem."

He stares gobsmacked at me. "Demons…"

"Yes. One of them tried to kill Dorothea. If

the men who attempted to do so had been mere mortals, I wouldn't be here. Fortunately, the demonic interference allowed me to intercede."

"I'm seeing things... would you mind doing that again?"

"How about something a little more difficult to dismiss as a trick of the eye?" I smile, then concentrate on him, casting a minor levitation spell. Its only true purpose is practicing witchcraft, since floating an inch or two off the ground isn't terribly useful beyond a party trick.

Isaiah emits a startled yelp, flails his arms as if he expects to fall, then stares down. "What have you done?"

"Levitation. The only safe way to get high."

He gives me a confused look. "I don't understand."

"It's pretty simple. Augustown has a demon problem. I'm not blaming you for it, merely warning you."

"God exists..."

I nod. "He and many other entities exist, like Gaia. The Devil. Jesus. Most entities humanity has revered as gods at one time or another do or *did* exist in some form. Once people stop believing in them, they tend to fade away. Except for the Creator. His existence doesn't depend on what humans think. Belief is relevant only to our dimension. Minor gods only exist here, for the most part, and don't cross sideways among different realities."

"Dorothea…"

"I'm only borrowing her body right now. You're not talking to Dorothea Povey, though she is still in here and can hear you."

He chuckles. "Wow. This is a lot to consider. Where do we start?"

I gesture at the house. "Probably with your wife."

"Queenie? What about her?" He takes my hand in both of his. "What are you saying?"

"She isn't doing anything wrong intentionally. Her abuse of laudanum to numb herself has given the demons a way into her mind. Your wife is still in the early stages of becoming possessed. Deep inside her thoughts, a battle for control is raging."

Isaiah stares at me. "What shall I do?"

"First step, I suggest you sanctify the church." I bite my lip. Not sure if I can technically help with that, but I *can* cast a protection spell to keep demons out. Not technically 'religious' in the sense he thinks of it, but the energy's coming from the same Origin, so… I can fake it. "Once the church is sanctified, we bring her there. If the demon's grip on her is weak enough, it will flee."

He nods once. "All right… Queenie, why

have you done this to yourself?"

"She misses her family too much to bear without the help of medication. You should know she must love you a great deal in order to subject herself to such emotional pain instead of leaving this place to return home."

"I see… perhaps I should listen to her and return with her to the East."

"She will be happier. I think you will, too."

Isaiah stands. "Then I shall do so. But *after* ridding this town of demons."

"Great. My thoughts exactly." I stand.

He looks scared.

Yeah, kiddo. It's not every day a person has their worldview kicked in the head.

Chapter Seventeen
Astral Projection

While Pastor Pearce runs to grab a book, I cast a minor protection spell on the church.

It's not going to last long, nor be too powerful. To really barricade the place against demonic incursion requires supplies I left home. Candles, incense, moon-blessed earth, some crystals... essentially stuff the pastor would in no way believe involved guardian angels. Well, the candles and incense I could probably get away with. Perhaps, if he's unfamiliar with witchcraft, he wouldn't recognize anything.

Still, I don't have any of it with me and there probably isn't a way to bring it here from the future. Not *too* important. Churches have been sanctified without the help of benevolent witches for a long time. Hopefully, he can figure it out.

When he returns carrying a large book, we enter the church. He goes right to the pulpit and recites a rite of sanctification. As far as I'm concerned, it's a spell, but that's a po-tay-toe/po-tah-to semantic thing. The only difference between spells and prayers is where the power behind it comes from. What's important is him believing it will work, and as far as my psychic abilities tell me, he does. Part of me thinks he'd been hoping for something to awaken him. Like, he'd lost faith and been regretting it... but just couldn't bring himself to get over one little hill of doubt without a little push.

I may be the first witch in the history of witchcraft to use a fireball to *save* lives.

Once he finishes the rite of sanctification, he insists I go with him back to the house. He knows Hosea is in jail and doesn't want me 'on my own.'

The instant I step through the front door, a bright white flash goes off in my face and I jolt upright in my Spirit Chair.

"Whoa…" I gasp.

Millicent appears standing in front of me. Sunlight in the windows tells me it's no longer almost two in the morning. I'm *me* again.

"Ugh. How long was I out?"

"Your vision ended in about ten minutes, then you fell asleep."

I rub my eyes, yawn, then rub my eyes again. "Felt like hours."

"Whatever you saw happened in the space of those first ten minutes. Sleep is sleep," says Millicent.

"Did I have a vision? It felt *so* real." I tell Millicent about how I seemed to become Dorothea, the demons, a whole town full of individual people who acted far too genuine to be products of my imagination. "Visions aren't active like that, Mills. They're like movies. This felt more like a video game I played rather than simply watched."

"Hmm. Yes." She taps a finger to her chin. "I believe you managed to astrally project yourself through time instead of physical space."

"Astral projection…" I tap my foot, thinking.

I've read about it before. Basically, it's like a person letting their ghost out of their body to go walking around. Chances are, I have the ability to do it, or at least the potential to learn. Astral projection is often associated with distant seeing. The CIA has reports of supposed distant seers who could astrally project themselves to a foreign enemy base and literally snoop around like an invisible spy. Only thing is… normally, the projection is in the real world, here and now.

"Yes." Millicent nods.

"But… astral projection doesn't leap across time, nor does it take people over. Did it really happen?"

She shrugs. "I cannot say. Though it is possible."

"Why Dorothea? How did I end up stealing her body and not Hosea's? I'd been concentrating on him."

"Had you been?" She smiles, raising an eyebrow. "I could tell you were heartbroken over what happened to that little girl. I think your focus drifted. The ragdoll is a powerful connection."

I look around for it. "Where'd it go? Did I drop it when I fell asleep?"

Millicent wanders around me, searching the carpet. "Hmm. Interesting. I don't see the doll. Perhaps the magic consumed it."

"Still doesn't explain why I possessed Dorothea."

"If the universe truly wanted you to act, you could've done no good inhabiting his body while he remained locked up." Millicent sets her hands on her hips. "She is his closest living relative. Not only had you been preoccupied with sadness over her death, the child represented the closest metaphysical anchor point to Hosea."

"Good point." I look around for the ragdoll, which appears to have vanished. Oh… wow. Inspired and highly curious, I sit back in the Spirit Chair and close my eyes.

"Now what?" asks Millie.

"Just some old-fashioned distant seeing."

I concentrate on the bottom of the shaft where I'd found the doll. The place left a strong emotional footprint on my brain, so it only takes me a few seconds for a vision of it to appear. Fortunately, distant seeing tends to ignore some rules of physics—like light. If an area is completely dark, it appears to me anyway, though in black and white. I think it's more me 'feeling' objects rather than seeing them. I zoom in on the ground, looking for the ragdoll… but what I find takes my breath away.

The bones are gone.

All the collapsed remains of the elevator are still there, but there's no trace of Dorothea's remains, a ragdoll, or rotten old ropes. I stare for a long moment at the spot where her smashed-open skull had been and get misty eyed.

I sit there stunned at the implication of changing the past. Dorothea's okay. Well… she at least didn't die that day from being thrown down a mine shaft. Her body no longer being there doesn't exactly prove my actions prevented her murder. It only proves the bastards didn't drop her *there* when/if they killed her. However, I can't help but feel as though she survived. It's sometimes difficult to tell wishful thinking apart from a psychic hunch, but I'm going to run with my hunch on this one.

Once the utter awe of affecting the present wears off, I end up blubbing like an idiot, overcome with joy. The ragdoll's gone because it wouldn't have been in the mine tunnel for me to find now.

"Don't celebrate too much yet, dear." Millicent squeezes my shoulder. "I pulled you back because you aren't going to be able to take on the Hangman alone."

I raise an eyebrow. "Why? Did you two know each other?"

She scoffs, arms folded.

"What? You *are* old enough."

Millicent waves me off, feigning offense.

"You're as old as you want to appear. You don't even have a physical body at the moment. *How* can it bother you to be called old?" I chuckle. "We're both ancient. Everyone is ancient. Souls keep going around and around."

She stops pretending to be annoyed just as the doorbell rings.

Huh. Don't remember ordering anything. "Great. Did I Prime while in a trance?"

Chapter Eighteen
Rule of Three

Despite feeling frumpy from sleeping in a chair, I head to the door.

"Close your bathrobe," calls Millicent.

Oops. I hurriedly pull it over myself and cinch the fuzzy belt before opening the door.

Ivy Tanner's standing on my stoop, staring at me like a teenager about to ask her mom if she can borrow the car. Sure, I'm older than her, but not by enough to deserve this look. I was ten or eleven when she came into the world. Far too young to be her mother.

"Hey," I say, stepping back. "C'mon in."

She darts past me the way Samantha used to rush out of direct sunlight. I shut the door, then turn to face her.

"Hi, Allie. Look… I messed up."

"Take a few breaths, calm down. Whatever it is, I'll help."

Ivy grabs my arms and stares into my eyes. "Nothing bad happened. I've had a change of heart, you could say."

"Oh?" I tilt my head.

Millicent walks up behind Ivy, smiling.

I blink. "Wait. Are you saying you don't want to quit the trifecta?"

She lets her arms drop to her sides. "I… the whole Jaguar god thing really freaked me out. I panicked. Everything was so weird and new and cool, then all of a sudden there's a massive stone giant trying to smash us on a boat."

"Something like that would rattle anyone." I chuckle. "I'm kinda worried it didn't break me, too."

Ivy paces around. "So, yeah… George reassured me helping Gaia is a worthy use of my abilities, and you guys need me. I'm done making evil movies though. Only going to be in nice ones, but… I understand witches aren't bad, and I have a real ability to help people. It would be wrong to ignore it or use it only for myself."

"Cool." I grin. "And there's no such thing as an evil movie… unless the director's sold his soul for fame and fortune."

"Wait… that's it? You're letting me come back?" She looks between Millicent and me. "Not going to make me beg?"

"Of course not." I hug her. "We're not *dark* witches. No weird initiation rites or taking pleasure in a sister's pain or desperation."

"See. I knew the universe would provide," says Millicent.

I peer around Ivy at her. "You knew?"

Millicent tilts her hand back and forth in a so-so gesture. "Not specifically it would be Ivy returning, but I suspected our trifecta would heal soon."

"You guys rock." Ivy squeezes me so hard I gurgle.

"Hey, easy. I don't need a Heimlich."

She laughs, then goes wide-eyed. "Oh, I had this crazy sad dream about some little girl being thrown down a hole in a cave. It felt way to vivid to be a nightmare. Not sure if it's a warning premonition or a ghost reaching out for help."

"Oh, yeah. It's a real doozy… but I've sorta got it handled." I scratch my head, ignoring the wild hair draped over my face. "Hey, would you mind doing me a *huge* favor?"

"Sure, anything," chirps Ivy. "What favor?"

I grasp her hand in both of mine, making

serious eye contact like I'm about to request she donate a kidney or something. "Please, go grab us some coffee. I just woke up and am in dire need of a shower. By the time you get back, I should be good."

She laughs. "You got it."

Chapter Nineteen
War Preparations

Ivy sits across from me at my kitchen table, staring at me in disbelief.

Crumbs from two egg sandwiches litter a pair of plates pushed off to the side. My coffee's gone. Hers is about halfway full—and I'd done most of the talking for the past forty minutes. She's fully up to date on everything regarding Vincente, Dorothea, Hosea, and my crazy experience giving the middle finger to the space-time continuum.

"Whoa," whispers Ivy. "That's super trippy. And *awesome.*"

"Millicent didn't believe I could handle taking on The Hangman by myself. I think it's time for me to bring some reinforcements and go back. Are you up for it?"

"Heck yeah." She nods so rapidly her sunglasses fly off the top of her head. "Much easier than a crazy Aztec god, right? No drowning. Heck, we're not even really there, so we can't die."

I shake my head. "We can't die, no, but… whoever we borrow could get hurt or die if we screw up too bad."

Millicent sips her not-tea. "Be wary. The demons can still destroy our astral selves if we aren't careful. Let me prepare a defensive spell for us first. The two of you should make the circle for our astral journey. We're going to need one to link ourselves and piggyback on your attachment to Dorothea."

"Does it matter the doll's gone?" I ask.

"It shouldn't, no." Millicent glides off to the mini nature shrine we've got set up on my balcony. "You still have a connection to Dorothea. I merely paused it."

Here's hoping. Still not sure if I sent myself there or if a guardian angel got involved. If *I* did it, no problem. Going back should be doable. If the angel's pulling strings, I pray they're watching and willing to give us another nudge.

Ivy and I grab a bunch of candles, crystals, and bowls of various magical herbs like mugwort, vervain, amaranth, and hemlock.

"Aren't you working tonight?" asks Ivy while we carry the stuff to the living room.

"Yeah."

"How long is this going to take?"

I set the armload of candles and the herb box down. "Well, the few hours I spent there passed as only ten minutes here. And I still have about three hours before I need to run out the door to not be late to the station. Should be plenty of time. Besides, this is a kid's life we're talking about."

We both sit on the floor.

"But didn't you save her already?" Ivy unrolls our giant witch mat.

It's kinda like a yoga mat, except for being made out of cloth and covered in a pre-embroidered ritual circle. Okay, it's not a mat at all. It's a queen-sized bedspread. Whatever. It works. Drawing a new circle for every ritual is tedious and time consuming. Besides, this keeps the wax off the carpet.

"It seems like I did, yeah, but I'm not talking about her literal life. More like quality of it. This girl's only got her father left. And he really loves her. She knows it, too. Like all the love she should be getting from two parents, he's giving her. If she loses him…"

"Yeah."

"They won't fire me for being late or missing one night. The way things looked, I don't expect Hosea has a lot of time. Two or three days at most before they kill him. I was there for seven to eight hours and only ten minutes passed here. There should be plenty of time to do what we need to do, and I still won't be late for work."

Ivy nods. "Now I understand why you sucked down two large coffees."

"Right?" I exhale and plonk down a few candles in their spots.

"Hey wait..." Ivy nudges me. "We're here now."

"Yeah, obviously."

Ivy smirks. "Not what I mean. We're already way in the future from what's happening to Hosea. Why risk your job? We're going back to the same place in time if this works, right? Let's do it after your show."

"There's no way I'm going to be able to focus on doing a show while I'm worrying about the Poveys." Plonk. Another candle.

"Wow, you're really worried about them." Ivy smiles. "I like that about you."

"You like I'm neurotic over people who lived 170 years ago?"

She sets out bowls of earth, water, and dried amaranth. "No, silly. I like how you're so

191

driven to help people you don't even care if it'll get you fired."

"I can find a new job. Dorothea's not going to be able to find a new father."

"Yeah, but he's already dead. Whether we leap back now, or leap back a few hours from now isn't going to matter for them, but I get you're anxious."

"Mmm hmm." I chuckle. "Guess I spent too much time being a little kid again. I want them to be safe *now* and I can't bear to wait."

Ivy laughs. "Now *that,* I can totally sympathize with."

"Well, you are a lot closer to being a child than I am."

She, rather maturely, sticks her tongue out at me.

An abrupt sensation washes over me like a million spiders doing the macarena. Judging by Ivy going cross-eyed at the same instant, it happened to her as well. Thankfully, the creepy full-body tickle only lasts a few seconds.

"I assume that was Millicent's doing?" asks Ivy.

I nod. "She's finishing her spell now."

On cue, Millicent glides in through the patio door, which she didn't bother to open. "The protection spell is in place, ladies."

"Great, so demons can't kill us now?" Ivy

peers up at her.

I set various crystals around the circle, working by feel. The same way moving two magnets close together makes them want to twist around so they attract, the crystals shift in my hand, seeking their appropriate places. My Mount Shasta crystal likes me, wants to be right in front of me.

"With this spell in place, it would be quite difficult for them to do so and impossible for them to attack our minds. However, my protection is primarily on our physical selves. This will prevent demons from following our astral trails back here and taking our bodies while we are elsewhere." Millicent floats down to sit cross-legged in her spot around the circle. "We should still be careful. The spell will give us some protection from charm and illusion, but if the demons decide they're going to get physical... it won't help much. Only our astral selves will be going there. My magic won't protect the bodies we inhabit. Well, you inhabit. I am purely an astral being and will remain so."

"Right." I hold a hand out to each of them. "Ready?"

"Yeah." Ivy grins. "This is so cool. Weird, but I'm not at all scared."

I give her hand a squeeze. "Makes sense. After *Tepēyōllōtl*, nothing else should seem too scary."

"If only." She whistles.

Millicent takes my right hand. Her fingers are neither warm nor cold, but solid enough to grasp. She's already pulling energy from me. Ivy shoots pointed looks at the candles, causing them to spontaneously ignite. Millicent does the same to the incense. I close my eyes, concentrating on the Mount Shasta crystal and thinking of it as almost a 'transmission antenna' that will send our astral selves into another place and time.

Okay, unknown guardian angel, if you're out there watching, any help you can give is welcome.

Both Ivy and Millicent have a mind link with me. Ivy's isn't as strong due to newness. It dropped for a while when she quit, but as soon as Millicent and I accepted her back into the trifecta, it reconnected. I suspect she hadn't completely dropped off, which explains why she dreamed about Dorothea. No doubt, it leaked from me. My feelings toward Sam not being a good fit for the trifecta surprise me. On some level, my soul mourns the loss of our old bond. But I'm also far happier to have Ivy back than I thought possible. It's totally like being told my younger sister died in a car accident only to find out someone made an error and she wasn't even in the car. No, I don't actually have a younger biological sister, but as part of our trifecta, Ivy is just as dear to me.

Sam and I are still best friends. Our souls still have a connection, even if it isn't through our witchy association. So yeah, no reason to be maudlin. The Universe needed Sam elsewhere, and, exactly as Millicent thought it would, it rebalanced things by bringing Ivy back to us.

Okay. Time to focus, Allie.

Dorothea Povey. Hosea Povey. I picture the little church next to Isaiah Pearce's house. I concentrate on Dorothea's emotional pain over losing her father, the fear she endured when those men discussed how to kill her right in front of her. Last, I hold my desire and need to make things right close to my heart. This started off as me thinking I needed to help a guy deal with an angry ghost in his house... but it's so much deeper.

Over our mental link, Ivy and Millicent pick up my thoughts and also focus on the same things. We synchronize our magic on a common goal. When I begin attempting to distant-see across time, Millicent adds to it by bringing her memory of astral projection forward. Ivy and I turn our meditation inward, visualizing our souls separating from our bodies, beooming spirit energy capable of following a pinhole conduit across space and time, guided by my laser focus on the events of Augustown 1849.

Another tingle ripples down the outsides of my arms. The sense of floating up out of my body feels like I'm taking off a hundred-pound winter coat I no longer need, yet Millicent and Ivy still hold my hands. The three of us drift in a sort of void together, then lurch downward, falling, still holding hands.

Hang on, kiddo. I'm on the way... and I'm bringing reinforcements.

Chapter Twenty
A Little Angry

My eyes open to the sight of a plain ceiling painted cornflower blue.

Just like Dorothea's eyes.

Early morning sunlight floods the small bedroom from its only window on my left. I sit up to take in my surroundings. I've once again 'landed' in Dorothea. My head's kinda stuffy like a lot of crying happened recently. I'm wearing a nightgown too big for me, but it's clean. Speaking of clean, so am I. Upon peeling the covers back it's obvious Dorothea had a bath before going to bed.

Wow! You came back! I was scared you left me.

You cried yourself to sleep?

Yeah. You disappeared, and Papa is still in jail.

Oh, whew. We made it in time.

To Dorothea, I think/say, For a second there, I worried the crying came from us being too late. Umm, how much time has passed?

It's the next morning. When you left, I fell to the floor. Pastor Pearce thought I fainted. He let me take a bath and borrow one of Mrs. Pearce's nightgowns. She washed my dress. It's hanging outside to dry. They're going to order me some new clothes. Augustown's so small, there aren't any other kids my age here. None of the tailors have dresses my size ready.

That's lovely of them to help you.

Yes and no. They think Papa's going to die, so they're expecting to take me in and let me live here. I'm very thankful, but it makes me sad.

Listen, Dorothea, I don't want to get your hopes up. This is entirely new for me. I don't know for sure we will be able to save your father, but I promise you, my friends and I will do everything we can. Don't give up yet.

Okay, I won't. And... your friends?

Remember what I told you yesterday about witches and some of us are good people?

Yes.

Well, witches work best in groups. Three is a powerful number. My two witch sisters should be here with me this time. Just not sure whose body they landed in. Heh. Maybe we'll get lucky and Ivy or Millicent took over the sheriff... or the judge.

Dorothea laughs nervously. *Pastor Pearce went back out to the church after he told me to sleep. I think he spent all night praying.*

Well, he had a lot to catch up on.

I was going to ask him why God let me die and Papa die and a bad man like Mr. Loughton get all the gold... but I didn't.

Why not?

A sense of the child smiling tickles the back of my brain. *Because Papa and I didn't die. Well, not yet. And you are here. I'm sure He sent you.*

Or at least your guardian angel did.

The door opens. A much-more-awake Queenie stumbles in. Her hair's nearly to her waist and completely wild. The poor woman's pale as a ghost and looks like she just ran a marathon after snorting a pound of cocaine while undergoing electro-shock therapy.

"Umm, Mrs. Pearce?" I ask, pretending to be Dorothea. "Are you all right?"

"It's me," says an unfamiliar voice, delicate and high. Queenie whistles while looking around. "Wow. This totally feels like I scored a role in a remake of *Tombstone*. Did you land in the kid again?"

"Yeah. Ivy?"

"Of course." Queenie/Ivy crouches in front of me, staring into my eyes. "Wow, she is adorable. Poor dear. Yup, that's the girl I saw—"

I cover Queenie's/Ivy's mouth. "She doesn't need to keep being reminded of how they, um, did away with her."

"Oh, right. Sorry." Queenie steps back, clasping her hands.

Your friend is in Mrs. Pearce like you're in my head?

Yes.

Please be careful. Pastor Pearce will be heartbroken if she is hurt.

Understood.

"Sorry it took me a few minutes to get here," says Queenie. "I had to give a freeloader the boot first."

"Freeloader?" I ask.

"Yeah. It's a pain in the butt to possess someone when they're already half-possessed. This woman had a demonic attachment forming I needed to cut off."

A cloud of inky darkness jumps out of the wall into the bedroom, rapidly coalescing into a solid creature about five feet tall, barely man-shaped. Its monstrous, somewhat-human face has no eyes or nose and a mouth three times the size of normal, lined with pointed silver teeth.

It growls.

"I think he's a little angry with me," says Queenie.

Dorothea screams.

Chapter Twenty-one
Plans

The demon leaps at Queenie.

Despite the distraction of Dorothea's terrified shrieking in the back of my mind, I gather enough concentration to project a force barrier, using it like a battering ram to shove the creature off course. Been a while since I used this spell, but if it's got enough power to smash a car, it'll knock a demon around.

Grr. I couldn't help that child any more than by avenging her death, but I am *not* going to lose this one.

Millicent—still her normal ghostly self—walks in at the same time the demon smacks into the wall. Queenie hikes up her huge nightgown and scrambles around behind the bed, valiantly putting me—presently a child—between her and the demon. Looks cowardly, but I understand. She's our kitchen witch. I'm the cannon. While I did manage to teach her how to cast a spell similar to my fireballs, she ended up making little more than tiny magic bolts. Energy darts, basically. Certainly not enough to stop a minor demon.

I'm sitting on the edge of a bed, my feet not reaching the floor… and I'm wearing an adult-sized nightgown. Mobility is not on my side at the moment. This garment is going to trip me if I try to run. Nothing like having my proverbial back against a wall for inspiration. I thrust my hands out again, casting the spectral bolt I used on Charles Clapp.

My 'ghost fireball' hits the demon low on the left, basically in its hip, leaving a tunnel through its fat bug-body as if I'd dropped a red-hot metal ball on a block of Styrofoam. The demon shrieks in agony, collapsing over to one side as I've destroyed its ability to stand. Hip bones are somewhat important for that.

Millicent rakes her hands at the air in a manner similar to a cat shredding its claws down the side of a couch. Spectral lines appear near the demon, tearing gashes into its back from invisible claws the size of a grizzly bear's.

Ivy's yellow energy blast sails past me on the left, nailing the demon in the side of the head. Black slime explodes all over the wall like she shot a watermelon point blank using a twelve-gauge. The rest of the demon's body disintegrates into smoke. Seconds later, the gore all over the wall disappears, too.

"There is one good thing about fighting demons." Millicent claps her hands in a 'dusting off' way. "Cleanup is easy."

Dorothea stops screaming. I get the sense she wants to curl up in a ball, hiding under the covers.

Shh, sweetie. It's gone. Looked scary, but not tough.

W-what was that?

A demon. The one my friend kicked out of Queenie. She's free of it now. I twist to look behind me at her. "Ives, you okay?"

"Yeah. Just arguing with this woman about her drug habit." Queenie/Ivy sighs. "Yes, you do have a drug habit. You *saw* the demon, right? Well, there ya go. How do you think it got into your head in the first place?"

I'm scared, says Dorothea. *Is it going to come back?*

Probably not. As long as Queenie can keep herself off the laudanum, a demon won't have a crack it can slip through. Besides, I think once we get this town sorted out, Pastor Pearce is going to take her back east so she isn't separated from her family. He didn't realize the extent to which being out here hurt her... and yet she stayed with him, so he knows she loves him. Once she no longer has a drug habit or depression to use against her, she should be safe from demonic attack.

That's sad. I hope she's happy. Am I going to have to go with them?

You're old enough to handle the truth, so I'll give it to you. There's a chance we might not be able to save your father. If we fail, you absolutely should go with them. If we *do* manage to get your father out of his current situation, you'll stay with him, of course. However, he really ought to take better care of you.

He takes fine care of me.

I poke myself in the ribs. You aren't eating enough. You don't have shoes. Love is amazing, but it can't replace food. He spends too much time digging and not enough time providing for you. I understand he's searching for gold out of a strong desire to give you a fabulous future, but he needs to balance his time a little better.

You said Mr. Loughton found gold in the mine real soon after he stole it from us. Is Papa going to find gold?

If Loughton did, there's no reason to think your father won't either. Here's hoping, kiddo.

"Okay, I've got this lady sorted. She's a bit freaked out at me taking her over, but willing to see where it goes." Queenie walks around to the side of the bed I'm sitting on. "So, Allie... umm... are we really going to be able to do this while you're stuck as a ten-year-old?"

I'm eleven.

"I'm eleven," I say in the same childlike, insulted tone.

Millicent laughs.

Ivy stares at me. "Seriously?"

"Yeah. Seriously. She's eleven, not ten." I fold my arms. "Doesn't matter. Her age isn't affecting my magic."

"Maybe not, but her age is affecting your attitude." Queenie/Ivy laughs.

I sigh. "It isn't like we need to get into fistfights with demons. Being small won't change anything. Besides, the three of us are together again."

"Okay." Queenie claps once. "Goals. What do we need to do here?"

Don't let them kill Papa!

"Our primary goal is to stop the town from executing Hosea Povey," I say. "Two men most likely working for this Claiborne guy killed a marshal and a local deputy. The town, no doubt due to Claiborne's influence, is blaming Hosea for it. Also, Claiborne's got a weird vibe. He might be the one summoning the demons."

Queenie taps her foot. "All right. So, we need to find some way to prove Hosea didn't do it."

"Dorothea saw them," I say.

"Yes, but they will accuse her of lying to protect her father." Queenie frowns.

"Also," says Millicent, "it sounds like the judge they call The Hangman is corrupt and taking money from Claiborne."

"Correct." I swish my feet back and forth under the nightgown. "Sure seems like it. Really, the man just wants the mine. Maybe I could talk Hosea into letting him have it?"

I don't think so. Papa said some really bad words to Mr. Loughton when he tried to buy it. The offer was too low. Papa thinks because Mr. Loughton wants the mine so bad there's definitely going to be gold in it. He didn't want to give it up for so little money.

Yes, but would he give it up for his life?

I hope so.

"Things may have already escalated beyond the point Claiborne is willing to back off." Millicent frowns. "A marshal and a deputy are dead. The town is going to want justice for the killing."

Queenie raises a hand. "They could always blame unidentified bandits. Works in movies."

"Maybe. But seems a little convenient. Not sure anyone will buy it. And I don't think the two killers would be willing to take the fall to spare Hosea." I hike the oversized nightgown up far enough to expose my feet. "I'm also going to need to collect her dress from the clothesline out back. This thing is far too big on me… her."

Millicent stops pacing, turning to look at me. "The two men who tried to hurt the child. You know for a fact they're the ones who killed the marshal and deputy?"

"Yes. Dorothea saw them do it. The lawmen came out to her home to speak to Hosea about something. She doesn't know what. Charles Clapp and another guy named Micah ambushed them. Then they grabbed Dorothea."

"Poor little thing," says Ivy.

Hey, I'm not that *little.*

Such a natural response gives me hope she's not going to be permanently traumatized by this, bringing a tear to my eye. "They came back for her the day after Hosea's arrest. Charles had a demon possessing him, but the other guy went along with the idea of killing her… which to me is worse. Demons are gonna do what demons do, but Micah had no issues murdering an innocent child so his boss could make money. His only hesitation was not wanting to make it painful. The man fully intended to kill her as long as it happened quick and painless."

"Ooh!" Queenie points at me. "You gave me an idea."

"I did?"

"Yeah." She snaps her fingers. "When you said you didn't think they'd take the fall to spare Hosea. I'll whip up a potion that'll make them unable to lie for two to three days... provided I can find the stuff I need." She gazes up to the side as if listening to someone on the phone. "Pharmacist might have it. According to Queenie, he's got all sorts of weird stuff."

"Probably because Claiborne is a dark warlock," I mutter.

Millicent holds up a finger. "Yes. I like this plan. Those two men *did* kill the marshal and deputy. A truth potion is an elegant solution. Get them riled up in public so everyone hears them admit what they did. Even a bribed judge would have no choice but to dismiss the case. A man like him will save his own skin before respecting a backroom deal."

"Perfect." Queenie nods. "Give me an hour or so to get the supplies and make the potion Allie, you're small and probably off their radar now. They'd gain nothing by hurting Dorothea at this point, so they'll leave you alone. Go snoop around. Try to find them, but don't be seen."

"Okay."

"Do those men know Dorothea saw them shoot the lawmen?" asks Millicent.

They didn't say anything about seeing me when they kidnapped me.

"Uncertain." I shrug. "Another group of lawmen arrested Hosea at the mine, so the sheriff didn't see Dorothea alive at home... or even bother checking on her. Charles and Micah went to the house the next day to get rid of her so they could blame Hosea for killing his daughter as well."

Millicent frowns. "I do not believe they realize she saw them. Call it a hunch. Keep quiet for now. No need to give them a reason to want to silence her. While you go looking for the killers, I am going to snoop around Claiborne's house, see what I can discover. The man has secrets. Perhaps I can find something we can hold over his head and force him to back off."

"Be careful." I slide off the bed to stand, nearly tripping over the nightgown in my attempt to take Millicent's hand. Grr. She's not solid at the moment. When my hand passes through hers, Dorothea gasps. "Claiborne Loughton is full of bad energy. He might be able to see you."

She's a ghost!

Yes.

Your witch friend is a ghost!?

She is.

Why can I see her? I've never seen ghosts before.

You're probably seeing her because I'm inside your head and what I think, you see. So *I* see her and you're sharing it.

All right. I believe I understand.

Ready to go snooping around?

I'm scared, but yes. We will need to get my dress first.

"Ives, would you please grab my—umm, Dorothea's—dress? I'm going to break my neck trying to go down the stairs in this thing."

Queenie heads for the door. "Sure. Be right back."

Chapter Twenty-two
Concessions

People in town still largely disregard my presence as I wander around peering into windows.

However, with Dorothea cleaned up and her dress washed, she—we—no longer look like a Depression era beggar child, likely the reason a few people who *do* notice us smile or say hello as opposed to everyone pretending we don't exist. Still, it's weird how little attention we get. This is hardly New York City where everyone's too busy to pay attention to a little girl wandering around alone peeking into windows.

I almost don't need to use magic for stealth.

Speaking of which, I have a spell that forces

people to ignore me. It's not literal invisibility, more like it encourages people to disregard my presence. The effect is entirely mental, so it doesn't do anything about cameras and sensors. Not a problem in 1849. Of course, this is the era of 'children should be seen and not heard... and preferably not even seen.'

To my modern sensibilities, I can't get over how I'm walking around looking like a little girl and no one thinks to check on me or even give me a long 'what's she doing alone' stare. This is a tiny town. Everyone here has to know who I am and where 'my' father is.

Dorothea tells me a little bit of random information about people we see, most of whom she thinks are reasonably nice. Stuff like Mr. French has six sons, Miss McDivitt recently lost her sister to sickness, Ms. Lemmon's husband died in the War of 1812, old Marian Applegart's gone a bit off in the head and talks to invisible people and so on. (No, I don't see any ghosts conversing with the old woman. Pretty sure she is actually suffering from dementia—or she seriously needs to stop wearing a heavy black dress in the sun.)

Anyway, Dorothea is used to being nigh invisible and feels lonely having no other kids her age around. There are a handful of *little* children here, none older than five, the offspring of shopkeepers and their new, young wives recently arrived from parts east. With Hosea working all the time, either in his mine or doing random jobs for people, she's been mostly on her own during the day after her mother left.

She doesn't think it odd she's able to walk around without being questioned as to where her parents are or why she's alone. Filling her head with too much information from the modern age might cause problems for her later on, so I try to keep it simple and explain how society has shifted. It's not like children are at much greater risk in the future. Certainly, the same amount of bad things happened to them even in 1849. In our time, society pays more attention to it.

Trying to hunt for the two killers as inconspicuously as possible, I peek in the windows of several shops, then the local doctor's office— eek. Hey, I'm an adult and the weird stuff in that place is going to give *me* nightmares. Old-timey doctor's equipment is straight out of horror movies. In a bizarre twist, Dorothea's not afraid of the creepy tools. Guess to her, they're normal.

Today, I don't call attention to myself by begging or trying to talk to anyone. Took care of that yesterday. Most residents of Augustown realize Dorothea is still alive and well while Hosea is incarcerated. It would take literal magic for anyone to believe he could hurt her from jail. The more I think about it, the less it sounds reasonable they killed her to ensure Hosea's conviction and more to simply be cruel or feed the demons. Blaming her father for it had been a convenient way to sweep it under the rug. Even in a time like this where the citizens are ambivalent to a little girl running around alone, if a child dies, people tend to lose their minds and demand justice. Kind of an odd paradigm, if you ask me. Can't be bothered to pay attention to the kids until something bad happens to them, then they get angry while ignoring the bad stuff might not have happened if they paid more attention.

Sigh. People.

Or maybe I'm being overprotective. I dunno.

Thank you for caring about me and Papa.

Fortunately, choking up with emotion doesn't interfere with my mental voice. No problem, kiddo. I'm just glad to be able to try.

You did more than try. You saved my life already. She giggles nervously in the back of my mind. *Are we really looking* for *the men who wanted to kill me?*

We are. They won't do anything to you in the middle of town with people watching.

And the demon's gone.

True. However, I think Charles is pretty evil to begin with. Didn't look like he had a problem with laudanum or booze. Something else had to give the demon a way in, and the something in question is most likely greed, desire for power, or a dark heart.

Upon reaching the saloon—probably should've gone there to start—I sneak onto the porch, crouching by one of the two front windows to peer inside, my nose even with the windowsill. The fragrance of paint, horse manure, and dust floods my sinuses. It's rather early in the day for people to be drinking, but the room has a light crowd of mostly older men. I spot Charles Clapp and Micah seated at a round table with four other men playing cards. Doesn't look like they're drinking liquor too heavily yet, but they're gambling.

My breath fogs on the glass in front of me. Staring through the heartbreaking, innocent reflection of Dorothea's face on the window at the two men who nearly murdered her almost pushes me over the edge of anger. If I'd been here in person, I might've shown them both what fireballs look like up close. Normally, I recoil from the mere thought of killing a person, but anyone who kills—or is willing to kill—a child no longer counts as a 'person' to me.

Technically, I *have* killed before, though not intentionally. That teacher, Mr. Fletcher, tried to run me over. I summoned a wall of force as a defensive measure to stop him from squishing me under his front bumper. He'd been going so fast, hitting it killed him. Okay, perhaps it's possible I hurled the wave of magic *at* him rather than merely erected a wall. The cops did find it somewhat confusing how he'd managed to get his car going fast enough to die instantly on impact. They also couldn't figure out exactly what he hit. Obviously, a magical force wall didn't even enter their minds. I'd played traumatized, saying I flinched away from the oncoming car and had no idea what he hit. But back to the important thing there—he died and I basically killed him. It doesn't bother me. He deserved to die. He *had* killed little Penny Laurie, and who knows what else he'd done to how many other kids. Charles and Micah only *tried* to murder Dorothea.

Dial it back a notch, Allie. Not going full *Terminator* here. Especially not while 'dressed up' as a child. Not only would Dorothea be forced to witness it, she'd be punished for it. I can't be responsible for her being burned alive as a witch or even hung.

"You son of a bitch!" yells a man behind me, a short distance off in the street.

Before I can even swivel my head to look, gunfire breaks out.

A loud *clack* comes from the wall above me as a bullet strikes the saloon.

Dorothea shrieks in my head.

I dive flat to the porch on my stomach, hastily invoking a luck spell to keep ricochets or wild shots from hitting Dorothea. Men scream in anger between the staccato report of six-shooters. Clanks, shattering glass, and people shouting in alarm come from all directions. I belly crawl toward the side, away from the chaos in the street. Bullets zing by overhead. A distant window shatters. More wooden *clonks* come from the saloon wall.

Hide! yells Dorothea.

Working on it!

A stray bullet pierces the barrel at the corner of the porch, two feet away from my head. Water pees out from two small holes, one on either side. I grab the porch edge and fling myself headfirst into the alley, slithering down the steps before dragging myself into the low space between the buildings. Flat on my front, I should be fairly safe, having an entire porch and a one-foot-high brick wall between me and incoming bullets.

Reflections in the windows of shops across the street give me an indication five men are

still exchanging gunfire. Hollow wooden tromp-
ing echoes on the saloon porch from everyone
inside running out to watch the show. Holy
cow, what's wrong with people? A gunfight is
not a damn carnival performance.

It's over in about thirty seconds. I push
myself up enough to peer over the porch floor.
Charles Clapp, Micah, and about nine others are
all outside, commenting on the shootout the
way most guys talk about professional sports.
From the sound of their conversation, three men
are dead, two wounded, and the crowd's mostly
talking about how lucky 'Barnett Musgrave' is
to survive, having spent the whole gunfight
standing out in the open. Apparently, the two
survivors were on the same side in the fight, and
managed to fend off an attack from three
outsiders who don't live in town. It's unclear
what started the violence, nor do I really care to
investigate deeper. I don't want Charles and
Micah to see Dorothea right here spying on
them, nor do I want Dorothea to see dead
people in the street.

*I've seen men shot before. It happens here
every week.*

Yeah, well. Children shouldn't have to see
such things.

Why not?

Speechless. Wow. I dunno. Never been

asked *why* before. Umm… because kids aren't supposed to see murder. It's wrong. It can mess you up inside the head.

All right. I suppose that's why Papa doesn't want me lookin' at the men when they've been shot.

Exactly.

I keep hidden. It takes about twenty minutes for the people above me to lose interest in the goings on in the street and return to their tables inside the saloon. Once I'm sure the two killers aren't going to see me, I abandon my hiding spot. Time to run back to the pastor's house and tell Ivy where these two guys are.

As soon as I stand up, I notice they've left the three dead men in the middle of the street.

Ack.

I mean, they're not gory or anything, just kinda lying there. Bloodstains on their shirts are about the extent of what I can see from here. No more disturbing than a theater actor pretending to be dead. Still, I know they're not acting. Dorothea isn't *too* bothered by it… which bothers me. Unfortunately, they're between me and the pastor's house. I really don't want to walk Dorothea within arm's reach of corpses… so I go the other way, intending to loop around.

We don't get far before a sudden, *bad* feeling hits me, strong enough to stop me in my tracks. Dread incarnate. I stare down at my—Dorothea's—foot, toes partially buried in the dirt road, waiting for the horrible thing to happen. No one is moving around near me, and I don't sense any demons close by, so I risk lifting my gaze off the ground. I really, *really* hate feeling like a helpless mouse being stared at by a hawk.

The source of the bad feeling is as obvious as a brick to the head as soon as I look around.

Claiborne's three-story home.

I'm at the town's only intersection, a mere three paces from the porch of the fancy house and didn't even realize it until the wave of fear hit me. As I take in the imposing structure, the supernatural mood shifts from doom to the sort of urgency I'd feel watching a friend fall through ice on a frozen lake. Without a second thought about approaching the house of evil, I scramble up onto the porch, going straight to the nearest window.

Dark violet curtains mostly block my view, but a one-inch gap lets me peer into a lavish parlor. The room is huge, littered with expensive wingback chairs, little tables, a sofa, dark hardwood everywhere, a fireplace.

Speaking of fireplace… Claiborne Loughton stands in front of it, holding a large, fancy crystal cylinder glowing like a dim fluorescent bulb. The sight of it sends a chill down my spine. I'm certain the light is coming from Millicent. This bastard has gone full *Ghostbusters* and trapped her in a bottle somehow. Now I understand why it feels like my friend is drowning in a frozen lake. Millicent needs help.

Crap!

I consider charging in and blasting the guy, but hesitate. Taking Claiborne on alone has 'bad idea' written all over it. Not to mention, I'm presently inhabiting the body of a little girl who hasn't been eating well. Allison Lopez the witchy adult has a fighting chance, but if he gets a hand on Dorothea Povey, it's over. I should go get Ivy. I start to turn away from the window, but stop short upon noticing the trail of dusty footprints I've left across the dark—and immaculately dust-free—porch. There aren't many people in Augustown running around barefoot, and no one else Dorothea's size. Claiborne is going to know I was here. Not sure how much of a problem it would be, but... dammit.

Worry pulls my attention back to the window. Claiborne appears to be studying the crystal cylinder, holding it up while staring into the light. I imagine Millicent giving him a piece of her mind whether or not anyone can hear her while she's stuck inside that little prison. The woman's too old-school for coarse language, but a dressing down from her scathes far more than any four-letter word could hope to.

What the heck is he doing?

I stand there on my toes, gripping the windowsill, watching, paralyzed by dread and worry. All Claiborne appears to be up to is observing the shimmering glow. Certainly, he won't be content to stare at her for long before doing worse. Dark wizards sometimes consume souls to power more elaborate rituals. Still not sure what this guy is, but he's definitely *something.* Dammit, Millie! What happened? How did you get trapped in a bottle?

The board under my left foot shifts from the weight of someone sneaking up on me.

Ack!

Before I can turn, a man seemingly comes out of nowhere and grabs me from behind, clamping a hand over my face. I hammer my heel into his foot, but Dorothea's neither heavy nor strong enough to faze him. He hauls me into the air, hurriedly dragging me in the front door to the parlor. As much as it's possible for me to move, I invoke every scrap of self-defense training in my arsenal, but he's so much bigger than me—Dorothea—all I'm doing is annoying him. In my flailing panic freakout, I can't even tell where his balls are to smash.

The dude clamps an arm around me, pinning my arms. I keep trying to kick… at least until Claiborne sets the Millicent jar on his mantel and walks up to us. His presence scares me, even though I'm not really a little girl. So dark. Up close, he's *worse* than a demon. The energy coursing through him is… infernal. As soon as I stop struggling and go limp, the man holding me puts me down on my feet and takes his hand off my mouth. He grabs a fistful of fabric at the back of my neck, cinching my dress tight around my chest, his knuckles digging in between my shoulder blades.

If I time it right, escape might be possible. It'll cost me this dress, but better the embarrassment of streaking across town than whatever this man is going to do to me—or I could start blasting. Do I fireball Claiborne and hope the big guy behind me doesn't smash me before I put him to sleep? Do I put him to sleep first and hope Claiborne doesn't pull a sword out of his cane and kill me? Using magic in front of him would reveal myself as a serious threat, not a harmless child. Problem being, *both* of these men could easily kill me faster than I could take them both out.

Run! yells Dorothea. *Drop down out of the dress, crawl through his legs and run!*

Can't. Too tight around the chest. I'd have

to rip it open.

So rip it! I don't care about a stupid dress. I don't want to die. Please get us out of here!

"Well, well, well..." Claiborne looks me over. "I must confess to being unsure what, exactly, you are... but you are definitely *not* Dorothea Povey. At least, you are not *entirely* her."

Dorothea's fear and small size are affecting me, too. Bad guys are way scarier when they tower over me. All I can do is stare up at him.

Claiborne leans his weight on his cane, flicking lint off his sleeve. "My associates tell me you did some rather amazing things, little girl. I had not been expecting that."

The shock of being caught finally settles enough for me to find a voice. "You're right. I'm not Dorothea, but this is still her body. You crossed a line when you involved demons."

He throws his head back, laughs briefly, then gives me this 'oh you poor simple creature' condescending smirk.

"There's no gold on Hosea's land," I say, narrowing my eyes. "I've seen what's there 171 years from now, and it's a forgotten hole in the ground."

"Of course there isn't any gold there *now*." He pats my cheek. "However, there *will be* gold there when my people look. It's in my contract."

I gawk. Whoa. Now I understand why he's giving off this energy. "You sold your soul to the Devil, didn't you?"

Claiborne leans back, muffling a laugh as though a high-society woman told a mildly bawdy joke at a social event. "Oh, don't fool yourself, who or whatever you are. No one in this country—or the world—has money like I have money unless they've struck a deal with *him*. Every politician with real power, every famous person, every man wealthy beyond reason... it all comes from the same place."

Grr. Not sure if he's lying, deluded, or correct. Regardless, it's pointless to get into an argument about it. I'm not here to save Claiborne's soul—which is probably an impossible task anyway at this point. The first step in saving someone is them realizing they need help. This guy's totally into the whole Team Satan thing. Time for a change of tactics.

"Okay... look. You want Hosea off the land so you can take the mine. There's no reason to have him killed. I can talk him into leaving if you agree to let him go."

He gives a faint sigh, half turning away. "Dear child, the time for reason has passed. Hosea Povey had the opportunity to walk away alive already, but he allowed it to slip from his grasp. His fate is sealed. The Hangman demands his due."

Oh, damn. He must intend Hosea's death as some kind of payment for his contract with the Devil. Eek. Is *that* why they tried to kill Dorothea? One of those strange bits of witchy insight hits me... he has to provide six souls a year.

Claiborne spins abruptly to face me. "This child is no longer important. Consider me sparing her to be as much of a concession as I am willing to make. Stay out of my way." He flicks his hand at me in an 'away with you' gesture.

Before I can get another word out, the dude holding me hauls me into the air by his fistful of my dress, carries me like a scruffed kitten out the door, and tosses me into a heap on the porch.

The door slams behind me.

I'm too surprised/relieved at not being killed to think about much of anything beyond running. I scramble to my feet and haul ass across Augustown and out into the surrounding desert, heading for Pastor Pearce's house. When I'm about halfway there, Dorothea starts sobbing. I slow to a walk, trying to help her deal with the crash of emotions. Fear, relief, and dread about her father's impending death swirl around in a messy tangle she's not mature enough to process all at once. Heck, most adults would have trouble dealing with a murderer teasing them then deciding on a whim to let them go while simultaneously knowing their father is about to die. Add the guy radiating tangible evil, and it's next level. Normal people wouldn't feel the negative energy. Kids and animals usually do. Witches definitely do. Dorothea's sensing it both from her innocence and from having me in her head.

I don't know if being inside a kid's mind is messing with me, or if it's her overwhelming emotion right now, but I can't stop crying over Millicent. It's no longer a question of what he plans to do with her soul. The man's not a dark witch… he's undoubtedly going to use Millicent's soul to pay the Devil when he has to. The few people I pass on the road don't react much to me going by. Of course, the sight of Dorothea in tears running away from town makes sense to them given Hosea's situation.

The problem here is far worse than I thought. Claiborne Loughton sold his soul to the Devil for wealth and power. Everyone in Augustown is in serious danger…

Especially my ghostly witch sister.

Chapter Tweny-three
Helping Hand

By the time I reach the pastor's house, my tears have stopped.

Anguish has given way to determination. Emotions are ruled by brain chemistry, and right now, my soul is swimming around in a bucket of eleven-year-old hormones. I'm kind of a sensitive sort of person to begin with, so being inside a kid's head is not helping me stay calm. For the same reason small children cry when they skin their knee, but an adult merely mutters a few bad words, I'm a wreck.

As soon as I recognize it's not *me* making my emotions go wild, I can get a handle on them.

I barge in the front door of the pastor's house. Queenie/Ivy rushes out to the parlor from the hall, already wide-eyed in fear since she's picking up my mood.

"What happened? Are you okay?" She fusses over me.

"Physically, yes." I grab at her hands. "I'm good. Stop treating me like a child."

A sad giggle interrupts Dorothea's quiet, constant sniffling.

"You *are* a child at the moment." Queenie winks. "Sorry, she's just so darn adorable. You look terrified."

I bow my head, sigh, and take a deep breath. "Claiborne trapped Millicent in some kind of... soul jar, I think. He's made a deal with the Devil—literally. I also think Judge Hangman is somehow involved in a supernatural sense. I'm not sure. Claiborne said something about the hangman needing his due."

"Claiborne's probably being melodramatic," says Ivy. "If he's truly made a deal with the Devil, he won't care who gets hurt as long as he obtains what he wants."

I pace, raking my hands through my hair. The sight of a little girl acting like an over-stressed office manager makes Queenie/Ivy laugh.

"Seriously?" I stare at her.

"Sorry. Again, adorable."

I growl. "Enough with the adorable crap. We have to figure out a way to get Millicent out of there before Claiborne does something to her."

Queenie nods. "Did you find the two men?"

"Yeah, but we have bigger—"

"Here." She hands me a tiny glass bottle no bigger than an adult man's thumb. "It doesn't look like much, but it's enough to split between them."

I take the bottle, which appears to be full of red-tinted water.

"Find a way to get them to drink it. They'll be compelled to speak only truth for two or three days. Give it about five minutes to take effect, then simply ask questions so they admit to killing the marshal and deputy... even trying to kill Dorothea."

I tilt the bottle in the light. "How am I going to walk up to two men who tried to kill me and convince them to drink a mysterious liquid?"

"Allie..." Queenie grips my shoulders, staring into my eyes. "You're not thinking like Allison Lopez. You're acting like a little girl who isn't a witch. Tricking people into drinking potions is Witchcraft 101. It's like *the most* stereotypical thing a witch can do. Give them the potion. Go find the sheriff and pretend to be

Dorothea. Tell him you saw the men shoot the marshal and deputy. When the sheriff goes to question them, they won't be able to lie."

She's right, of course. Worrying about Millicent is making my head spin. The two goons are in a saloon. It should be easy to get them to drink a potion, especially if they don't know they're doing so.

"Right. Okay." I rub my forehead. "I'm on it. What about Millicent?"

"I'm sure all sorts of chaos will break out when the lawmen confront the killers. It'll give me a distraction to go in there and grab the jar."

"Lawmen? Since when do you talk like that?" I laugh.

"I'm in character." Queenie fans herself. "This is honestly the most detailed set I've ever had the fortune to perform on. All the extras are on point. No one has broken character even once... though I'd seriously stab someone for some Starbucks right now."

Heh. I'd find her act more amusing if we weren't on the verge of losing Millicent and Hosea.

"Queenie?" asks Isaiah as he strides into the room. "What's going on here? Why are you acting so odd? What is a star buck?"

"Never mind." Queenie points at me. "Don't go anywhere. Be right back." She darts down the hall.

"Pastor," I say. "I'm back. Dorothea's taking a nap right now."

"The angel?" He blinks.

"Angel?" Queenie laughs from the other room. "Oh my."

Isaiah gives her (well the hallway) side eye.

Queenie rushes back in and hands me a hunk of bread and some cheese. "Here. She needs to eat. We stole her right out of bed in the morning. That poor girl is just skin and bones."

I set the potion on the table nearby and chow down as fast as possible. She's right. This kid needs food.

"Pastor, listen," I say in between bites. "I've figured out why everything has gone crazy here. Claiborne Loughton has made a deal with the Devil. He's not a dark witch or even a summoner. The man's fully given himself over in exchange for wealth, power, and influence. This entire town and everyone in it is at risk. The darkness will consume everything it touches. I've seen the future. Merely a hundred years from now, no trace of Augustown will remain."

"Well..." He rubs his chin. "A lot of these towns popping up now are just people searching for gold. They don't find any, people leave. Towns fall apart. What's happened to my wife? Has she been burdened with so much grief she's lost her mind?"

"No." Queenie fans herself again. "I'm not your wife right now. I'm… another *angel* here to help get the demons out of Augustown. By the way, you're welcome."

"For?" Isaiah blinks at her.

"Your wife's laudanum habit allowed a demon to infest her mind. There's only so much space in here. My arrival forcibly removed it. Once we are finished here and I take my leave, her mind will belong to her again."

Listening to Ivy talk like that—words, inflection, tone… she fits right in here. Yeah, I think she did have a minor part in a western movie early in her career (straight to DVD, but still). If I remember right, she played the teenage daughter of either the local judge or the beleaguered rancher. Her role mostly consisted of standing there fretting about everything and saying 'whatever are we to do' repeatedly.

A cinematic masterpiece, it was not.

"So… there's someone inside Queenie's head?" asks Isaiah.

"Yes," Ivy and I reply simultaneously.

"Don't worry, she's quite all right with the situation." Queenie smiles. "The poor woman was losing her battle with the demon and is rather grateful it's destroyed."

Isaiah takes her hand. "Wife, I cannot in

good conscience leave this place while so much darkness remains, but I give you my word, once the demons are sent back to the pits of Hell, we will return to New York."

Queenie winces.

He leans back, alarmed.

"Oh, don't take it the wrong way." She smiles. "Queenie is still here as a voice in my head. She squealed in delight when you said you'd take her back east, nearer her family. Loud. Also, she wishes me to say she loves you dearly."

"Her staying with me despite her pain proves this." Isaiah starts to lean in for a kiss, but stops. "I shall wait to show my affections in a more physical manner until such time as my wife is her own self once more."

Queenie nods.

Isaiah looks at me. "How I can I help?"

"By holding down the fort—"

Isaiah holds up a holy book. "No. I will not stand idly by while the forces of darkness march upon the Earth. My doubts are laid to rest. I cannot claim to understand the way in which He works, but I understand now my thoughts have been clouded. I will stand with you in this hour of need."

Ivy thinks, *He might not have magic, but the demons could very well respond to sincere faith.*

I nod at her. "I'll go find our 'friends' and make sure they take the potion, then get the sheriff involved."

"And I'll go with Isaiah and try to recover Millicent as soon as we have the opportunity."

"Who is Millicent?" asks Isaiah.

"She is our spiritual guide. Another angel, but in noncorporeal form." Queenie smiles. "The nefarious rogue Claiborne has imprisoned her."

I stare at her. Really? Laying it on a bit thick, are we?

She waves dismissively. "All right. Places everyone." Queenie claps twice. "Let's do this."

I look down at myself, raise and lower my toes. Be nice if I was a little more *Lara Croft* and a lot less *Little Orphan Annie,* but it's what I've got to work with.

Sorry, Miss Allison. I do not understand what you mean.

Heh. It's all right. You shouldn't understand those references. Means I am worried about your safety going into 'battle' as a little girl without any weapons... or even shoes.

Pastor Pearce is having some made for me. They'll be ready in a couple days. We don't need weapons, only truth. Because we're not lying.

Oh, the idealism of youth. Sometimes, a girl needs truth plus a big stick. Since I don't *have* a big stick at the moment, we'll make do with sneaky.

Are you ready? I ask her.

Yes. They wanted to hurt me and they killed two lawmen. You said they won't hurt me when people are watching. I'm not scared. No, I shouldn't lie. Miss Allison, I am scared a little... but not enough to hide.

You're a tough kid, Dorothea.

Will you tell me how they were going to kill me?

I think about finding her bones as a reflex to the question, failing to stop myself.

Eek! She shivers mentally. *I've always been scared of the mine. I don't even like looking at it. Every time I see the hole in the hillside, it feels like it wants to hurt me.*

Hmm. Wonder if she's got a little sixth sense ability? Did some part of her psyche know she'd meet a bad end in there? No matter. She's not going down that shaft.

"Let us be on our way then," says Isaiah. "Yea, though I walk through the valley of the shadow of death..." He heads out the door, reciting scripture.

Queenie/Ivy follows.

I pick the little bottle up off the table and

examine it. Looks like red water, but it's giving off a noticeable magical tingle. It's good to have our kitchen witch back. Determined not to let Claiborne hurt Millicent, I run out the door, race past Queenie and Isaiah, and keep on running all the way to Augustown.

Chapter Twenty-four
Breaking the Rules

I'm out of breath by the time I reach the downtown area.

My eagerness got the better of me, but the faster we do this, the less likely we are to lose Millicent. Our trifecta has shrunk momentarily to two, but we've got Isaiah's help now.

At the edge of town, I slow to a walk. A stagecoach rumbles in from the north, coming to a halt in front of the largest of the general stores, the one with a US Postal Service sign in the window. Augustown's too little to have a dedicated post office, so I guess the shopkeeper handles it.

I dodge the occasional horse, group of

women, or disappointed miner. No one pays any attention to the little girl striding along with a look of mission in her eyes. They probably think I'm playing some imaginary game or acting weird due to grief. Perhaps being cleaned up and no longer filthy keeps them from worrying if I've had anything to eat.

The dead men are thankfully gone from the street, though the undertaker's wagon is still there. Looks like he and his worker *just* finished loading the last corpse. Cringing, I look away and step into the saloon. The crowd's noticeably thicker than even an hour ago. My heart skips a beat when I don't see Charles or Micah around at first... Aha! They've only moved seats. Same table, but they've got their back to the room.

Whew.

Dorothea's confidence falters. The sight of the two men who almost threw her down a mine shaft has her second guessing any desire to be within sight of them.

Shh. Relax. I got this.

I raise my right hand and weave a spell around myself. Nothing visible happens except for a faint magical breeze making my hair flutter momentarily.

What did you do? I feel strange. You're doing magic again, right? I felt how you think of spells.

Yes. It's a hiding spell. As long as we don't touch anyone or make noise, people won't realize we are here. It's kind of like being invisible.

Ooh, really?

Yep. Watch this.

I approach a table, standing in plain sight of an older guy. He's staring right at me when I stick out my tongue and make a silly face at him, but doesn't show the slightest reaction to me being goofy.

Dorothea laughs, then emits a gasp of awe. *Wow. It really works.*

It does, but it's not perfect. If I touch him, he'll see us. Okay, no time for play.

I stand by a column to avoid accidental collisions, observing Charles and Micah playing cards for a little while, debating sneaking up on them and spiking their drinks. Unfortunately, the men have empty glasses in front of them. Oh, I know… easy fix for that.

Slow and careful, I pad across the room to the bar and slip behind it.

No! We're not allowed back here.

Please deal with it just this once. Sometimes, minor rules need to be broken for the greater good. Going back here doesn't hurt anyone. But you're right. We shouldn't be here.

I have to climb up to kneel on the counter in order to reach two tumbler glasses and a bottle of whiskey.

Eep! Don't touch liquor! I'm going to get in trouble.

Your dad have a thing against liquor?

No. I'm too young.

Then don't worry. We're not going to be drinking it.

Moving as fast as I can without spilling, I empty Ivy's potion into the glasses, dividing it as evenly as possible before adding a healthy amount of whiskey. I stretch to put the bottle back on the shelf, hop down off the counter to my feet, and grab the two glasses. Hmm. Don't want to leave the tiny potion bottle there... so I pick it up in my teeth.

Josep McKeney nearly walks straight into me. I flatten myself against the counter, hands —and whiskey glasses—stretched out to either side, leaning back as he reaches for a bottle on a high shelf. His stomach hovers an inch from my face. Dorothea emits a faint gasp of fear, worried about making him angry and getting in trouble. To her, not only are we in a place we don't belong (behind the bar) we're stealing whiskey.

I hold still like there's a four-inch murder wasp on my nose.

Josep takes a huge green bottle down from the top shelf, carrying it off to pour someone a shot.

Whew.

I slip out from behind the bar and navigate the maze of tables and chairs over to the left side of the room. Charles and Micah are still playing cards at the big, round table. Six other men are in on the game as well, though I can't tell by looking at them if they're Claiborne's henchmen or simply random locals. Fortunately, the two killers are seated next to each other. I turn sideways, stretching one arm out to set a whiskey glass on the table by Charles Clapp's cards with all the care and precision of a tech defusing a bomb. After extricating myself from the narrow space between the men's arms, I turn the other way and stretch to set a glass down near Micah.

He fidgets unexpectedly in response to being dealt a bad card, and bumps my arm.

Eep.

I yank my hand back as he turns to look. Ducking low, I scurry off to the right. Micah swats Charles, starting a minor argument. 'Stop poking me' 'I didn't touch ya' goes back and forth for a minute before they get over it.

Dorothea's shaking from nerves.

I retreat to the back corner of the saloon, pluck the little bottle out of my mouth, and hide behind an empty table where I can watch the men. While staring at them, I focus my desire on them.

"Drink," I whisper, infusing my words with magic. "Drink… drink…"

Charles and Micah appear to notice the whiskeys at the same time. They look around, clearly wondering where the glasses came from.

"Drink," I whisper again, louder. *"Driiiink."*

The men exchange a glance, shrug with a 'don't look a gift whiskey in the tumbler glass' attitude, and pound the drinks in one gulp. Wow, damn. Those two are serious about their booze. I had to have poured at least two or three shots' worth in each glass.

Are we done breaking rules now?

Yeah, kiddo. I hope so. Time for part two.

Chapter Twenty-five
A Whole Lot of Convincing

Ivy said it would take about five minutes for the potion to kick in.

As much as I'm torn up with worry over Millicent and in a hurry, I force myself to *walk* out of the saloon. Once outside, I release the magic keeping me concealed. Bad idea to seemingly come out of nowhere in the sheriff's office. Despite no longer having an enchantment forcing people not to pay attention to me, people still largely ignore me.

Suppose Dorothea should take it as a compliment. If people didn't trust her, they'd be staring at her, expecting thievery. She becomes increasingly nervous as we draw nearer to the sheriff's office. Hosea shoving me away the other day has her terrified of how the lawmen will react to her being there. I try to calm her down by pointing out that walking in the front door to talk to the sheriff is totally different from having an unauthorized conversation through a window with a prisoner they aren't allowing to have visitors.

Like most buildings in the downtown, the porch is covered in dust thick enough for me to leave footprints. Only Claiborne's house had pristine, dark polished wood. Of course, my feet had been so dusty I still left tracks on it. Makes me wonder why anyone would bother going to the trouble of cleaning it to such a degree of perfection.

Three wanted posters hang in a large window to the left of the door below gold-painted letters spelling out 'Sheriff.' I approach the black-painted door, peer in the window at a few men sitting around behind desks, and grasp the little knob. Their conversation peters out to silence as I walk in. They all stare at me, surprisingly not in a hostile manner. One man looks down, seemingly guilty. The other two look pitying. Other than having badges on their shirts, they're dressed in the same manner as every other gunslinger and cowboy here.

Dorothea mentally points at the oldest guy,

probably in his late thirties. *That's Sheriff Rupp.* She shifts her attention to a man with short light brown hair. *Deputy Witters. The other man is Deputy Travers.*

Travers appears to be the youngest, still in his twenties. He's also part Mexican, if I had to guess.

I run over to the Sheriff's desk. A carved-wooden block at the front edge bears the name Wilson Rupp.

"I'm real sorry, hon," says Sheriff Rupp. "Can't let ya down there to see him. Got a few miscreants around ain't fit for a delicate child to be in the company of."

I open my mouth, then catch myself before speaking. Need to play the role. "Sheriff, there's been a big mistake."

"Mistake was your old man shootin' Marshal Nye and Deputy Dublin," mutters Travers, in Spanish.

Grr. I have to ignore him since Dorothea doesn't know Spanish.

Sheriff Rupp, however, raises his eyebrows. "Oh? What sort of mistake?"

Witters folds his arms. He seems to expect I'm here to try talking them into letting Hosea go by making stuff up, but he doesn't give off annoyance. More like 'yeah, figured sho'd do this, poor kid.' Of the three lawmen, he seems the most sympathetic.

"Papa didn't hurt anyone," I say. "He was working in the mine when the marshal and deputy came by. I saw two other men attack them. Wasn't Papa."

The sheriff and deputies exchange a look.

"You know, hon, it's against the law to lie to us," says Witters. "I understand you're trying to save your father's life, but you go on and run off now. We'll pretend you didn't say nothin'."

I hold eye contact with Sheriff Rupp. "The same two men came by the house next day after you took Papa away. They tried to kill me, too. Was gonna throw me down a hole in the mine, but I got away. I just saw them in Mr. McKeney's saloon right now, playin' cards. One's named Charles Clapp. He called the other guy Micah. Don' know his last name. But they're there right now."

"You sayin' they tried to hurt you?" Sheriff Rupp walks out from behind his desk. He takes a knee in front of me so we're about eye level. "You're making a serious accusation, Dorothea."

Sheriff Rupp is nice. He likes Papa. He knows I don't lie about nothin'.

"Yes, sir. I know." I hold up my arm, which still has a little bit of a red mark from the ropes. Dorothea had been struggling pretty damn hard to free herself before I popped into her head.

"Why'd they want to do a thing like that?" asks Travers.

"I heard them talkin' about it. They tied me up and were tryin' ta figure out how to kill me so's you'd all think Papa did it and you'd be extra irate with him and make sure he got hung."

Witters approaches and grabs my left arm around the bicep. "She's tellin' tales to save her old man. Maybe a night in a cell will teach her to respect the law and not fib."

"I'm not fibbing. I swear I saw them shoot Marshal Nye and Deputy Dublin. I was right in the house when they did it. *Please* at least go question them before they get away."

Witters doesn't look impressed. Sheriff Rupp sighs, head bowed.

"You know Papa wouldn't kill anyone, sheriff." I pull on his arm. "Those men killed the marshal and the deputy and just left them there to be found. If Papa did it, why wouldn't he hide the bodies in the mine? He could have made it so no one ever found them. If someone fell down a deep shaft and died, no one would ever know what happened to them."

Dorothea shudders.

Witters raises an eyebrow. "Hmm. She does bring up a point. Why'd he leave them out there to rot?"

"Remember Steckman," says Travers, glancing at the sheriff.

Who or what is a Steckman?

Mr. Steckman is Mr. Loughton's lawyer. No one really talks directly to Mr. Loughton. Everyone does business through Mr. Steckman.

The sheriff rubs his chin. "I remember. His word against the girl's."

Witters folds his arms. "Loughton and Hosea have been feuding for months. Wouldn't put it past Steckman to lie for Loughton."

"And a frightened daughter wouldn't lie for her father?" Travers gestures at me. "Damn right Hosea and Claiborne have been at odds. Finally pushed the man over the edge. Hosea wasn't in his right mind when he shot Marshal Nye and Deputy Dublin."

I stare at him. "Everyone in town saw Mr. Loughton speaking to Judge Boothe. I heard Ardelia and Gretchen say the judge took money from him. Mr. Loughton wants to steal Papa's land. He sent those men to kill the deputies and make it look like Papa did it. Mr. Steckman is tellin' lies."

"Just hold on there a moment, girl." Sheriff Rupp raises a hand. "How would Mr. Loughton have even known Marshal Nye and Dublin would be there so he could send men to ambush them?"

"Umm…" I blink. Dorothea's drawing a blank here, too. Time to think. "Why did the marshal want to talk to Papa?"

"Delivering papers," says Witters. "Hosea had been summoned to appear before Judge Boothe on a dispute of land claim… filed by Claiborne Loughton. Steckman had gone with the marshal and Dublin out to the property the day of the shooting. He barely survived."

Travers' disbelief melts to an 'oh, wow' expression.

"See?" I peer up at Sheriff Rupp. "Mr. Loughton knew the marshal and deputy would be there to deliver the papers. His own attorney was with them. Charles Clapp and Micah ambushed them by the house and left the bodies out in the open on purpose for you to find. I was inside the house. They didn't know I saw the whole thing."

Sheriff Rupp and Deputy Travers came to the house not even an hour after the shooting. I was still hiding under my bed.

"Steckman says he barely escaped with his life. Came right here to get us," mutters the sheriff. "Possible Hosea left the bodies there, not havin' the time to drag them out of sight."

"Papa wouldn't kill them and go back to work in the mines," I say, grinding my toe into the floor.

Witters sets his hands on his hips, frowning. "Kinda odd to do that, now she brings it up. What kinda person would shoot two men in cold blood, then go right on back to work?"

"Foster Steckman *did* go with Marshal Nye and Deputy Dublin to serve the court papers," says the sheriff. "He works for Loughton. He arranged for the papers to be served. I suppose it's remotely plausible he might have been aware of an ambush."

"Foster told us your old man came out the door shooting." Witters frowns.

I thrust my hands out to either side. "Think! If Papa was out of his mind with rage because of his fight with Mr. Loughton, don't you think Mr. Steckman would've been the *first* person he shot? How did he, Mr. Loughton's right-hand man, walk away without a scratch, but both the marshal and Deputy Dublin are dead? The man who told you about the killing works for Mr. Loughton who has been trying to steal Papa's land for months. He's set everything up."

The sheriff and two deputies keep looking back and forth at each other. Seems they're starting to ask questions but stalling on a 'yeah, she's probably right but we can't do anything about it' attitude.

"Please at least go question the two killers.

You're a sheriff. You can tell if someone's lying."

Dorothea's supplying plenty of fear and emotion. I've never really been the sort of person who falls to pieces when losing an argument. Even as a kid, I didn't throw tantrums or cry over stupid crap. However, this isn't 'stupid crap.' Her father's life is hanging in the balance here. Ack. Bad turn of phrase. I mean, her father could die. Sheriff Rupp is definitely sympathetic to Dorothea, and I think he's about as close to a friend as Hosea has in this whole town. Between the emotional storm going on from Dorothea and my memory of how I felt when discovering her remains in the mine, I break down in tears.

They're about thirty-five percent acting.

"Please!" I pull at the sheriff's shirt. "Papa really didn't hurt anyone. He didn't fight when you arrested him. He's not crazy with anger."

Sheriff Rupp picks me up into a hug. "There, there, girl. Easy. No need to get all emotional. All right. I'll at least go talk to these two."

"Girl, you're willing to swear in front of the judge you saw those men shoot Marshal Nye and Deputy Dublin?" asks Witters.

Sniffling, I wipe my eyes. "Yes, sir. It's the truth."

Sheriff Rupp sets me back on my feet and grabs his hat. "All right. Let's go see what they have to say for themselves. Travers, keep an eye on the office, will ya?"

"Sure thing, sheriff." He returns to his desk, leans back in the chair, and puts his feet up.

"C'mon, girl." Sheriff Rupp heads for the door, waving for me to follow.

Witters waits for me to go first.

Come on Ivy… please let your potion skills kick butt.

Chapter Twenty-six
Liquid Truth

Sheriff Rupp and Deputy Witters walk down the street toward the saloon.

It's not as dramatic or epic as one might expect. We're not on our way to the O-K Corral. Real life doesn't have stirring music in the background. I spot Queenie and Pastor Pearce lurking fairly close to Claiborne's house among a group of people chatting in the street. Queenie /Ivy glances at me as I follow the lawmen. I'm trying to keep my head down and pretend to be Dorothea.

Awesome work, says Ivy over our telepathic connection.

Yeah. I started to get a little out of character

there at the end. Got a little lawyery on them. The sheriff probably thinks Dorothea's smart beyond her years.

Well, I'm not dumb. Dorothea mentally sniffles. *Might've thought of those things you said if it wasn't Papa's life on the line.*

Kinda interesting, the sheriff doesn't seem to be on Claiborne's payroll.

Sheriff Rupp doesn't trust him, says Dorothea in my head. *He doesn't like 'big city' folk. Mr. Loughton's from somewhere fancy. Heard he's got a wife and baby there, still. Didn't want them to come to Augustown until he'd built it up proper enough. At least, that's what Papa said.*

I get a feeling the sheriff wouldn't have lasted too much longer after Hosea's death if he kept resisting bribes. They would either run him out, or worse.

Kill him, too?

Maybe.

The three of us walk down the dirt road to the saloon. The ground's uncomfortably hot, forcing me to take short, fast steps so I don't burn my feet. Reaching the shade of the saloon porch is a welcome relief. Everyone inside goes quiet when the sheriff and deputy walk in, most turning to look at them.

Sheriff Rupp hooks his thumbs in his belt,

gazing over the crowd.

I lean around him, pointing. "There they are."

The sheriff nods, leads the way to the men. I follow behind. When Rupp stops at the table, I say, "Those are the two men who killed the marshal and deputy."

Charles Clapp laughs. "Don't listen to the brat, sheriff. She's telling the truth." His smile dies in an instant to a stupefied expression.

"Idiot." Micah swats him. "What my associate here means to say is, we killed the marshal and deputy. I mean, we *did* shoot them. Uhh, we were absolutely there when they died." He breaks out in a sweat.

The room goes quiet.

Sheriff Rupp rests his hand on his weapon. "Charles Clapp. Micah Hine. Am I to understand the two of you are hereby confessing to the murder of US Marshal Heath Nye and Augustown Deputy Amon Dublin?"

"Yeah!" yells a red-faced Charles, while shaking his head to the negative.

"Why are you sayin' that, Chuck?" shouts Micah. "We're supposed ta lie. We shot both of them."

I point again. "They tried to kill me, too 'cause I saw 'em an' they didn't want me tellin' no one."

A handful of people gasp.

Telling anyone, says Dorothea. *I know proper how to speak.*

Sorry. Getting into the Wild West role a little too deep.

"Naw, we's just gonna kill her 'cause I like ta hear the little ones scream," says Charles before clamping a hand over his mouth and going wide-eyed.

"We had ta send a message. No one crosses Mr. Loughton." Micah nods. "He told us to make it look like Hosea Povey did it."

All the saloon patrons gasp in shock.

I step forward. Sheriff Rupp grabs my shoulder to hold me back. "Did you want to kill me because the demon told you to, or are you just bad?"

Charles points at me, laughing, shaking his head as if to say 'get a load of this kid.' He's trying to play it off like I'm lying, but blurts, "It was the demon's idea but I liked it. No, I mean, I was definitely going to kill the kid." He, too, starts sweating hard. "Naw, this kid's not making up stories, Sheriff. In fact, I killed a whole family a few months back in Montana territory 'fore the demon came around."

"We killed for the money!" yells Micah. "Claiborne paid us a hundred dollars each ta kill them law men on Hosea's land. We wasn't just tryin' ta scare her. We were gonna to kill her, too."

The men exchange the most epic of WTF glances.

Grr. Well, at least I don't have to feel bad for him going to jail. The demon didn't force Charles to murder anyone.

"Shut yer damn dirty mouth," roars Charles, then adds, "We had every intention of murderin' that child."

"Hell's wrong wit'chu?" barks Micah. "We s'posed ta lie."

Sheriff Rupp and Deputy Witters draw their revolvers.

"Charles Clapp. Micah Hine, you boys are coming with us. Real slow now, let's have them guns."

"Wait, wait, wait." Charles Clapp's eyes bug out. "It's *exactly* what the girl says. We killed those lawmen. But it *was* our fault. Gah. Yes! I mean… I was possessed by a demon, but I would'a done it anyway. Argh. There's evil in town, sheriff! Claiborne made a deal with the Devil and there are demons here. One's even got the pastor's wife."

"Crazy drunk fool," mutters a man a few tables away. "Don't know what he's even saying."

"He's right. Devil's with Claiborne." Micah

points at the wall. "We's gonna kill the little one 'cause Mr. Loughton got so angry with Hosea for not givin' up his land. But the kid got away. We can't kill 'er now on account o' everyone seein' 'er 'round town what with Hosea in the pokey."

"They tied me up," I say. "They were gonna take me into Papa's mine and drop me down a deep shaft so I break my neck and die. No one would ever find me, and everyone would think Papa killed me."

Another gasp comes from the room. The other six guys at the poker table gingerly get out of their seats and back away to either side.

"You *can* believe her." Charles jabs his finger at me. "She's *not* just sayin' this to get her daddy outta jail." He grabs his face and lets out a manic scream. "Why am I saying this?"

"She's gotta be a demon, too." Micah makes a cross with his fingers at me. "Threw fire outta her hands. Knocked Charles clear on his ass, then did some kinda voodoo what made me sleep. It's how she got away from us 'fore we could kill her. And we was definitely going to kill, in case that's not clear."

Sheriff Rupp and Deputy Witters exchange a 'these two are crazy' stare.

"You didn't tie me up too well. I got loose and ran away while you argued how to kill me."

I fold my arms. "You probably fell asleep because you drank too much."

You just lied, says Dorothea.

A little lie, yeah. If you start telling people you've got a witch inside you, they're going to think you're crazy. Sometimes—not very often —but sometimes, good people have to lie. Most people can't handle truth like this, about magic, or angels, or anything beyond what they think they know about the world.

Oh. All right. I understand. People would think I'm crazy if I said such things.

"Demons are everywhere." Charles, wide-eyed, points around the room. "Any one of you might be possessed. Claiborne brought the Devil himself to Augustown. He's going to take all of you with him."

Uh oh. He's acting out of his mind on purpose. He must have figured out something is preventing him from knowingly lying, so he's trying to say the wildest sounding things he believes to be true. If there's any doubt over his confession due to people considering him insane, I'm sure Judge Hangman will decide to kill all three of them, these two *plus* Hosea.

"He's lying!" I yell. "Pretending to be crazy because he confessed before he could think to lie."

Charles points at me again. "Will you shut

that damn kid up. She keeps runnin' her mouth, tellin' the truth. Claiborne told ya to stay away. Now, you're gonna get hurt, brat."

"Go away, sheriff," says Micah. "You know damn well Judge Boothe is in Claiborne's pocket. Whole damn town is. Cross him, it'll be you in a shallow grave."

Sheriff Rupp narrows his eyes. "Nice and easy now, you boys leave them guns of yours on the table and step away."

Charles stands up slow, gingerly grasps the revolver on his belt, and eases it out of the holster.

"Go ta hell!" shouts Micah.

The two men whip their guns up to fire.

Dorothea and I scream at the same instant. I thrust my arms out, reflexively conjuring the same force wall that saved me from being run over in the parking lot of a school. Sheriff Rupp and Deputy Witters start shooting. Four revolvers spit lead as fast as the men can shoot them. A man tackles me from the left, knocking me to the floor and covering me with his entire body.

It's over in less than ten seconds.

The bodies of Charles Clapp and Micah Hine thud to the floor.

Fortunately, the force wall I made only existed for a moment and is essentially hardened air—totally invisible. It's gone before anyone touches or notices it.

The man who pounced on me rolls off to the side, sitting up and looking me over. "You all right, kid?"

I don't recognize him, but he's a brave and good man. "Yes, sir. Thank you."

He's the captain of the fire brigade.

Fire brigade? He's a fire fighter?

Yes, Miss Allie.

Makes sense.

We stand at the same time. I only glance far enough toward the table to see four boots. Oh, hell. Maybe seeing them dead will help Dorothea not have nightmares about them coming to kill her for the rest of her life. What they did to her—even if it had only been tying her up and tormenting her by saying how they're going to kill her—would scar anyone.

I want to see.

All right. I cringe, but look toward the table. Charles and Micah lay slumped unceremoniously on the floor, Micah propped up against one table leg. They appear to simply be passed out drunk, except for their eyes being open, staring into nowhere. A few red spots mark their shirts, not gory at all, really. Blood expanding into a puddle on the floor below them is the worst part.

Dorothea squirms. *All right. Please look away now.*

I do.

Sheriff Rupp shakes his head at the two idiots.

Deputy Witters appears to be confused by the sight of flattened bullets on the floor—incoming fire from the killers that hit my force wall. No way to know if their hasty shooting would've struck the sheriff, deputy, or me… but it doesn't matter.

A crowd gathers on the porch outside, people rushing over to check out the gunfight. This is the Wild West version of traffic slowing down to ogle an accident. Josep hurries over to pull me away from the dead men. He brings me behind the bar where I can't see anything, treating me like the little girl I appear to be.

Dorothea doesn't mind the comfort, so I keep playing the role while mentally doing all I can to reassure her everything will be all right. Those two confessed in the middle of a crowded saloon—and are now dead. They even implicated Claiborne in the plot. Wow, Ives, your potion *did* kick ass.

I think we might have just spared Hosea from the noose.

Only thing to worry about now is Millicent, and it's a big worry.

Claiborne is *not* going to be happy when he hears what happened.

Chapter Twenty-seven
Due

A deafening banshee scream of anger comes from the street outside.

It's loud enough—and unearthly enough—to bring the entire saloon to complete silence. Yeah, no way in hell did such an eerie, amplified shriek come from any human lungs. A few seconds after the scream fades, the voice of Pastor Pearce bellows outside.

"… in order that Satan may not outwit us. For we are aware of his schemes!"

While everyone stands around in bewilderment, I dart out from behind the bar and rush onto the porch. Claiborne Loughton stumbles in a drunken stagger across the intersection away from his house, holding his head as if in great pain. Isaiah Pearce and Queenie/Ivy walk after him, the pastor holding up a book. Queenie's attacking him with a banishing spell. It has no visible 'special effects,' but every time she flicks a hand forward, Claiborne stumbles as if shoved by a big man.

A barely visible Millicent hovers outside the fancy house, twelve feet off the ground. Her long red hair flutters wildly; the rage in her eyes makes her look like The Morrigan, the Irish war goddess. I half expect to see a storm of ravens come out of nowhere and peck Claiborne down to his bones in seconds.

Across the street, almost right across from where I am, Judge Salem Boothe calmly stands on the porch of one of the few private residences in downtown, observing the goings-on with a dispassionate expression.

"When the unclean spirit has gone out of a person, it passes through waterless places seeking rest, but finds none," recites the pastor. "Then it says, 'I will return to my house from which I came.' And when it comes, it finds the house empty, swept, and put in order. Then it goes forth and brings with it seven other spirits more evil than itself, and they enter and dwell there, and the last state of that person is worse than the first. So also will it be with this evil."

Claiborne screams, "You will regret—"

Queenie glares hard for an instant. Her voice fills my mental link, calling on the Moon Goddess to banish evil spirits. An invisible force knocks Claiborne into a stagger and sends his violet derby flying.

Isaiah raises a hand. "And the Devil, who deceived them, was hurled into a lake of burning sulfur. That same lake into which the beast and the false prophet had been thrown. There, they shall know torment day and night for ever and ever."

"Stop!" yells Claiborne. "You blather nonsense!"

Queenie hits him with another banishing spell. Claiborne nearly falls on his face, flailing his arms for balance.

Heavy footsteps walk up behind me.

I peer back at Sheriff Rupp and Deputy Witters.

"Now ain't that a sight, Donnie," mutters the sheriff.

"True enough." Witters spits to the side.

"You all right, Dorothea?" asks the sheriff.

"Yes. I'm sorry those men tried to shoot you."

Sheriff Rupp shakes his head. "Damndest thing I'd ever seen. What got into them they confessed. Never seen no one 'angry confess' before." He chuckles. "Way they screamed and carried on, sounded like they's tryin' ta deny everything, but they admitted it."

Isaiah raises a crucifix. "Behold, I have given you authority to tread on serpents and scorpions, and over all the power of the enemy, and nothing shall hurt you. Unclean spirit, I cast you out from this child of God so that you may do no further harm here!"

Claiborne wails in pain, dropping to his knees. Frothing, he crawls forward, eyes wild like a caged animal. Ack. Exorcisms are almost impossible to make work if the person being oppressed wants to keep the demon. Then again, he isn't possessed. Doing an exorcism on someone who's sold their soul is probably only going to hurt.

"Am I seein' things?" asks Deputy Witters, "or is the Good Word causin' that man physical pain."

"Sure seems like it." Sheriff Rupp hooks his thumbs in his gun belt.

"Think those two fools back there were right about the whole soul-sellin' business?" asks Witters.

"God help us if they were," mutters the sheriff.

Millicent makes a whipping motion. Clai borne cries out in agony, though nothing visible passes between them. Oh, she's pissed. I'd help but… my fireballs are too damn obvious. Everyone would see a big glowing thing fly out of Dorothea into Claiborne. Besides, the three of them seem to have this under control. At least, as much as possible. No idea what they intend to do beyond torturing the guy for a while. Maybe run him out of town?

"Please believe me," I say, trying to do a childlike 'Dorothea voice.' "Papa was in the mine when those men were shot dead. Mr. Loughton wanted Papa's land."

"Eh…" Sheriff Rupp pats me on the head. "I reckon you're telling the truth, girl. Hosea don't seem the type to kill a man over a deed. And those two did admit what they done, then tried to shoot us."

Witters glances over at him. "There's no way on God's green Earth we'll prove Claiborne's involved with the killing. But we ought'a cut Hosea loose."

"Yeah, reckon," says the sheriff before spitting to the side, missing the edge of the porch by an inch.

The instant the words leave his lips, Judge Hangman shoots us a disapproving glare as if he can hear from across the street.

Claiborne Loughton clutches his chest, twitches once, and collapses in the street.

Pastor Pearce and Queenie stop in their tracks, seeming bewildered. Millicent lifts her head, staring down at him imperiously. A brief flicker of spectral energy flashes beneath Claiborne before disappearing into the earth.

The sheriff and Deputy Witters run—along with a bunch of other people—over to check on Claiborne. The sheriff stoops to examine him, standing back up two seconds later and shaking his head. All the men around him remove their hats, covering their hearts.

Judge Salem Boothe frowns at Isaiah Pearce, then disintegrates in a whorl of black vapor. I'm pretty sure I'm the only one who sees him disappear. Well, only living person. Millicent's eyebrows can't get any higher.

Queenie hikes up her dress and runs over to me. "Are you okay? What happened to Loughton? Did we do that? Oh, God, tell me we didn't kill him."

"No," I whisper, eyeing the empty porch across the street, "the hangman always gets his due."

Chapter Twenty-eight
Long Story

Sheriff Rupp emerges from the door at the back of the office, a smiling, crying Hosea behind him.

Papa! Oh, thank you, Miss Allison! Thank you!

Pure joy wells up from Dorothea.

You're welcome, sweetie. I have to go now. Be ready to have your body back. Don't fall over this time.

Goodbye. She sniffle-giggles.

The room floods with bright light. I catch a fleeting glimpse of the little girl running forward away from me into her father's arms before reality fades to white. Dorothea's shout of "Papa!" echoes like it came over a concert speaker system, rattling my brain. For a few brief seconds, it feels as though I'm flying along a tunnel at twice the speed of sound. A wall of energy comes up fast. I don't even have time to think 'oh, crap' before crashing into a spongy mass.

I find myself sprawled on the floor of my Beverly Hills apartment. Ivy's in the midst of a reverse somersault.

Millicent appears in a blast of spirit energy.

"Oh, wow," I say, holding my head. "What a ride."

"Ouch," mutters Ivy, landing in a heap.

"What hurts?" I ask.

"Yes."

We laugh.

"Did we win?" Ivy sits up.

"I think so. Hosea's released and Dorothea isn't going to be murdered at age eleven. Hang on. I gotta know." I drag myself upright and concentrate on distant seeing the mine.

The bottom of the vertical shaft looks the same as before, broken decaying wood and dirt everywhere—but no bones. Whew. I pan outward, phasing through solid earth to the outside world. Whoa. None of the mining company buildings are there. No conveyor belts, no fence, no rotting warehouses. There's only this tiny one-room shed. Holy sheep-nuggets! It's Hosea's little house! The same one I saw in the background out of Dorothea's eyes when those men had her tied up outside. Down the road a bit, instead of the big Loughton Mining sign, there's only a dinky six-by-eight-inch plaque on a stick. I zoom in on it.

Povey Mine Site – Kramer Junction Hist. Society.

My mind swims, trying to fathom the extent to which we just changed things. I shift my view east a few hundred feet. Vincente's house looks the same as before. His white Ford pickup is still there. Okay, whew. Didn't change *too* much. Hmm. I probably shouldn't call him again. If we really did alter the past, then Hosea's ghost would not have been haunting him, so he'd never have called my show for help. Talk about trippy. If I review the recording, is his call going to still be there? It's strange I don't have any memory of someone else being the last caller on that show instead of him.

Releasing my psychic eyes, I sit up and explain what I've seen.

"Trippy," mutters Ivy.

"That's what I said." Laughing, I stand into a stretch. "Wow, what time is it?"

"A little after one in the afternoon. You still

have plenty of time to make it to work." Ivy grins.

I pantomime wiping sweat off my forehead. "So weird."

"How much do you think we changed?" asks Ivy. "I mean, other than what happened to Hosea and Dorothea and the mine?"

"Not as much as you might think," says Millicent. "Lifetimes end when a person has done everything they've come here to do in a particular lifetime. You know this already. The means of death doesn't matter. The man who owned the house before Vincente still died on the same day. They found him face down on his kitchen floor next to a trash bag. Hosea's ghost had not directly killed him. The choking sensation brought on a heart attack. Some other cause set off the heart attack now."

I wonder how Millicent might know all this; then again, she's a ghost. Lord only knows what information she has access to. I nod. "So, the other three people who died on the property still all died on the same dates, but not because Hosea tried to choke them."

"Correct." Millicent fixes her hair. "To soothe your mind, Ivy, we did not kill Claiborne."

She exhales. "Whew. Good to know."

Millicent neatens her hair—not the way we

do, she merely thinks about it and it moves. "Alas, Hosea Povey never did find gold in the mine. He kept looking for only a few weeks before giving up entirely on the mine and focusing on various jobs, so he had the means to provide for his daughter. When Augustown dissolved, Hosea went with Dorothea to what is now Los Angeles. By then, she'd become a young woman. She married three months after their arrival in the city."

"So we *did* we change things," says Ivy.

Millicent nods. "Of course. Think of it this way. We put their lives back to the way they should have been from the start, the way they would have been if the demons had not interfered."

"I like that." I grin. "Good way to put it."

Ivy elbow nudges me. "You're thrilled because you saved a child's life."

"Yeah, can't argue that." I flop on the couch. "It's only 1:28 p.m. and I'm ready to go to sleep."

Ivy sighs. "The Old West was a rough place. I wonder how long she survived."

"Well, she at least made it to marrying age... which was what? Sixteen back then?" I roll my eyes.

Millicent chuckles. "Not quite that bad, dear. She married at nineteen, made it to sixty-four."

Ivy blinks. "Wow. Pretty good for back then."

She also named her first daughter Allison."

"Aww," coos Ivy.

I'm too choked up to speak, so I don't even try.

After a few minutes, I sit up. "Guess what, ladies?"

"What?" asks Ivy.

Millie turns to look at me.

I thrust my arms up to either side. "The trifecta is back together!"

Ivy squeals in delight. We bounce around like a pair of teenagers who just scored tickets to... whatever boy band teens these days are into. Even Millicent joins in. To be a wiseass, she makes herself look fourteen while acting childish.

Our celebratory moment comes and goes, leaving the air practically glowing from good energy.

Ivy abruptly stops grinning and stares at me. "Umm, Allie? Do you think Judge Hangman was the Devil?"

Millicent folds her arms. "Took you long enough to work that out, dear."

Ivy shivers.

"I admit, I didn't realize right away either...

mostly because the guy didn't throw off *any* bad vibes. Claiborne felt like pure evil."

Millicent shakes a finger at me. "The Devil, dear. He can hide himself. It's the scariest part of what he is. No one ever knows he's there until he wants them to."

"Crap!" Ivy shivers. "Are we going to have to fight him now?"

I wince. "No, but… we might have to worry about his replacement."

"Huh?" Ivy tilts her head. "What?"

"Uhh…" I fidget at my hair. "It's a long story. Won't finish it before I have to leave for work."

"At least give me a teaser trailer." She winks.

"You know my friend Sam?"

"Yeah."

"Did you know she carries a sword called the Devil Killer?"

"I think you mentioned it once."

"*Why* do you think it's called that?"

Ivy stares. "Oh, crap. Really?"

Millicent floats up to me. "Not to change the subject, but you forgot to scratch your lottery ticket, dear."

"Oh, all right, fine." Since we're acting like giddy teenagers, I overact 'attitude' and flounce into the kitchen to grab the lottery scratch-off she insisted I buy before all this craziness began. "You know those luck spells are borderline charlatanry, right?"

She merely looks at me.

Sighing, I pull out my keys and scrape the ticket… and win $500,000. I look at it, look away, look back at it—still showing the win—look away longer. It's still showing a win when I dare to peek again.

I scream, nearly fainting.

Millicent smiles a knowing smile.

"Are you playing with me?" I shake the ticket at her. "This is an illusion, right?"

She shakes her head.

Ivy zooms over, peers down at the ticket, smiles. "Yeah, looks legit. Nice."

Of course, to her, $500k isn't terribly impressive. She made like two million from just her last movie, not counting residuals. However, it's enough to keep me from freaking out over paying the rent for a while.

"Oh, damn." I slouch.

"What's wrong?" asks Ivy. "You're supposed to be happy. You saved the kid, got Hosea out of jail, beat the devil, and you just won some money."

I hold the ticket up again. "Threefold return. This is good luck. Something *bad* is going to happen to me to balance this out. We got this winning ticket because of magical luck. It's going to swing back."

"Yes, but not too badly, I think." Millicent twirls hair around her finger. "You're not consumed with greed, merely the desire to survive comfortably."

Whud!

The whole apartment shakes.

Sounded like a garbage truck crashed into the front of the building.

"What the hell?" I blurt, flailing my arms for balance.

Yeah something hit us hard enough to make the floor shake.

Ivy and I run to the front door. A trail of black smoke coming down out of the sky leads directly to my Honda Accord in the parking lot —or at least the spot where it should be. There's no sign of my car. Only a mangled jet engine sitting in its place. Fortunately for my neighbors, the spots around my car are empty.

"Ack!"

"Look!" Ivy points up.

A 737 or some sort of similar big airplane limps across the sky overhead, smoke peeling off the middle of its right wing.

"Oh, no," I whisper. "Please let them land safely."

"They will," says Millicent. "Frightened, but

unhurt."

I stare at my car, crushed like a soda can on a highway. "This is why I don't like using magic to get money."

"You're still coming out way ahead. Even after they take taxes out, you can easily buy another car." Ivy nudges me. "I'll give you a ride in today. Hey, why don't I hang out with you at the station? Maybe do an interview. Promise I won't flake out this time."

"Heh. Thanks. And great idea! Wasn't your fault. You had a little possession issue." I chuckle, then head back inside. "I should probably call 911."

"Good plan," says Ivy, before bursting into laughter. "Never a dull moment with the trifecta! Wow, I am glad to be back!"

And I'm glad you are. I'd say I hope Dorothea has a great life, but she's already been dead for over a century. Hmm. Wonder what she did with her life?"

"911, what's your emergency?" asks a voice from my phone.

"Hi, yeah… a jet engine fell out of the sky and smashed my car."

Silence.

"Yes, I'm serious. I know it sounds absurd, but I'm staring at it now. I'm afraid it's going to start a huge fire. Can you please send

someone?"
My life.
Can it get any weirder?
Wait, no. I should never ask that.

The End

About the Authors

J.R. Rain is an ex-private investigator who now writes full-time. He lives in a small house on a small island with his small dog, Sadie. Please visit him at www.jrrain.com.

~~~~~

Originally from South Amboy NJ, **Matthew S. Cox** has been creating science fiction and fantasy worlds for most of his reasoning life. Since 1996, he has developed the "Divergent Fates" world, in which Division Zero, Virtual Immortality, The Awakened Series, The Harmony Paradox, and the Daughter of Mars series take place.

Matthew is an avid gamer, a recovered WoW addict, Gamemaster for two custom systems, and a fan of anime, British humour, and intellectual science fiction that questions the nature of reality, life, and what happens after it.

He is also fond of cats.

Please visit him at: www.matthewcoxbooks.com

Made in the USA
Middletown, DE
29 December 2022

20578927R00172